CROSS MY WEREWOLF HEART

HEART

Hope Not to Die

For my husband, Steven.

You're without doubt the best person I know, and you get me in ways nobody else does.

*You humour me when I'm being irrational.
You support me when I'm down.
You make me laugh when I want to cry.
And you love me, and all my quirks, foibles, and weird obsessions, unconditionally.*

How many times have you watched Ghostbusters or Buffy the Vampire Slayer, just because you know they make me happy?

How many times have you listened to my questionable music choices, or gone to concerts you wouldn't otherwise be caught dead at, just because you know I love it?

You are my one true; my Rock God—my everything—and this one's for you.

•

In loving memory of my father-in-law, Benny, and sister-in-law, Louise. Always loved. Always remembered. Always in our hearts.

Series Overview

In the Cross My Werewolf Heart trilogy, Digital Content Manager, Clarissa Hunt's life takes an unexpected turn when she awakens in a body bag after a bizarre accident claims her life. But death is just the beginning of her wild journey.

Tasked with unraveling the mystery of her newfound immortality, Clarissa finds herself thrust into a supernatural world teeming with werewolves, ancient secret societies, and perilous enemies determined to end her life, for good.

As she navigates Melbourne's paranormal underbelly, Clarissa's sense of humor becomes her most valuable asset.

Amidst the chaos, she finds herself caught between a ruggedly handsome yet abrasive stranger, and a charming and alluring doctor, both vying for her romantic attention.

A tale filled with twisty turns, mayhem and mystery, Cross My Werewolf Heart, will have you turning pages faster than xxx, and leave you breathless with anticipation.

•••

Prepare to be enthralled by this fast-paced paranormal romantic comedy set against the backdrop of Melbourne, Australia.

With a comedic flair and a contemporary tone, Cross My Werewolf Heart blends otherworldly shenanigans with laugh-out-loud moments, providing readers with a captivating and entertaining tale.

Join Clarissa on her hilarious and perilous adventure as she confronts monsters, uncovers ancient secrets, and discovers that even in the face of danger, laughter can be the ultimate weapon.

If you love reading Robyn Peterman, MaryJanice Davidson, Cynthia St. Aubin, Carrie Pulkinen and Janet Evanovich, you'll adore sinking your teeth into Esther Del Zuanne's, debut series, Cross My Werewolf Heart.

Cross My Werewolf Heart
Hope Not to Die

"Have I ever mentioned how much I hate body bags?"
—Clarissa Hunt, Cross My Werewolf Heart: Hope Not to Die

•

I'm getting so sick and tired of dying.

I'm also getting pretty sick of all the werewolf mercenaries snapping at my heels and getting stared down by an uppity underworld receptionist who I'm pretty sure is a hell beast.

With my new ability to commune with the dead making me jumpier than a long-tailed cat in a roomful of rocking chairs, I'm pretty sure the end of my tether zoomed past me days ago.

At least the paranormal pains in my butt have stopped trashing my house.

With help (sort of) from my new band of not-so-merry sidekicks—Vincent, the immortal leader of the Patrons of Order, Poppy, the ghost of my dead twin sister, and Azrael, my imaginary childhood friend who, as it turns out, not so imaginary—I discover a diabolical plan to resurrect (pun intended) a forbidden experiment to create a master race of human-paranormal hybrids. A plan that was supposed to have been benched in the 1800s!

Still no closer to discovering how I ended up with a werewolf heart beating in my chest, I turned to my trusty friend, the internet, for answers.

Big mistake.

Not only did I not find out who was conducting the clandestine, inter-species transplant experiments, or how I got mixed up in the whole sordid affair in the first place, but I also unwittingly uncovered the red market: an online hub where paranormal body parts are bought and sold.

Nasty.

It doesn't help that my brain is all fuzzy with tingly thoughts about a certain smart-mouthed peacekeeper, and a dreamy cardio thoracic surgeon, both of whom are proving to be very distracting.

Perhaps meeting the werewolf and vampire elders at a super-secret meeting of the Patrons of Order would shed some more light on my dire situation?

I mean, it couldn't get any worse, could it?

•

Cross My Werewolf Heart: Hope Not to Die is the second book in the fast-paced, raucously funny and wildly unpredictable Cross My Werewolf Heart trilogy featuring sassy Digital Content Manager, Clarissa Hunt, and set in the fantastical world of #fangsfurandfreaks

Be warned, though, there's another juicy cliffhanger at the end of this book, and you simply won't be able to stop yourself from finding out the truth behind Clarissa's werewolf heart!

DISCLAIMER

G'day!

Just a quick note to let you know that, despite being published in USAmerican English, this book contains lots of fun Australian content. It's written by an Australian author, featuring (mostly) Australian characters and is set in Melbourne, Australia.

There are plenty of Aussie turns of phrase, references to Australian celebrities, sporting heroes, retail stores, and places that may be unfamiliar to readers who have never lived in, or visited Australia. These are integral aspects of the story and contribute to its unique charm and fresh flavour (yep, that's flavour with a U #winkwink).

I sincerely hope you enjoy this wild trip Down Under.

ONE

HAVE I EVER MENTIONED HOW MUCH I HATE BODY BAGS?

No, seriously, they're stupid and stiff and get all up in your grooves like heavy-duty cling wrap and they sweat like a bitch and aren't at all comfy.

I guess, in Paper Pak's defense, they probably never factored user-comfort into their design prototype. Why would they? It's not likely their average client would leave a shitty review on Amazon if the body bag wasn't comfy, is it? Unless they're me. I was quickly becoming a body bag aficionado and had practically turned coming back to life into an art form.

Speaking of which, know what I hate just as much as body bags? Bloody hearses, that's what. Because:

1. there's absolutely no head room in the back
2. the safety belts designed to keep the gurney in place don't hold for shit, and
3. the latch on the tailgate, not so latchy.

How do I know all this? Because, after dying in that shitty alley, I once again came back to life in a body bag, only this time I was in the rear of a hearse, coasting down the M80.

How was this my life? *How*?

Of course, because I'd become intimately familiar with how to unzip a body bag from the inside, that's exactly what I did, and then tried to sit up. Only, I couldn't sit up because I was strapped into the gurney by the aforementioned shoddy seatbelts.

After a little wriggling, the seatbelts gave way and I tried to sit up again. That's when I discovered just how little headroom there is in a hearse, because I whacked my head so hard on the roof, I saw stars. Literally.

Naturally, I let fly with a litany of colorful profanities that would have made a bikie blush, which is precisely when the driver, much like the orderly at the hospital, completely lost his ever-loving shit and promptly fainted at the wheel, sending the hearse careening off the highway and into a steep embankment. Apparently, he just wasn't accustomed to seeing passengers sit up and scream bloody murder in the back of his wagon.

Fair enough, too.

The jolt from the accident caused the shonky tailgate to pop open and the gurney that was no longer strapped in place thanks to my wriggling, shot out the back like a rocket, coming to a bumpy stop in the middle of the freeway.

Inbound.

During peak hour.

Let's just say, there was a mad scramble on my part to get out of the way of the oncoming traffic bearing down on me like it was, well, peak hour.

Talk about a close call, which if you think about it, was kind of ridiculous. If getting whacked in the head by a hockey puck, having your throat ripped out by a 300kg werewolf, or being eaten alive hadn't been enough to kill me, it was quite unlikely being struck by a car was going to do any permanent damage, either. But old habits die hard it seems, and my self-preservation instinct kicked in, even though, for all intents and purposes, I was pretty much immortal.

I wasn't aware the police had arrived until a tall man, dressed in a dark-blue uniform and matching Victoria Police baseball cap, stood in front of me, and asked if I was okay.

How had I not noticed the red and blue flashing lights? Or the wailing siren?

I blinked up at the officer.

"I'm sorry, pardon?" I said.

"Are you alright? Do you need medical assistance?"

I shook my head. I didn't need a doctor. I needed a bloody exorcist is what I needed.

"I've radioed for an ambulance."

Of course he had.

"It's on its way," he said.

Noooooo. No. No. No. I didn't need nor did I want any more medical professionals coming at me. I'd well and truly had enough of that.

"You okay to answer a few questions?" he continued.

I nodded and gingerly rubbed the lump that was growing on the top of my head where I'd smacked it on the roof. Stupid hearse. Maybe I *should* see a doctor? Maybe I was in shock? Maybe I had concussion? Maybe all the dying again and again was killing off my brain cells?

"What's your full name, please?"

I blinked a couple of times. "Clarissa Josephine Hunt," I answered, not really giving the officer any real face time.

"Thanks," he said, scribbling in his notebook. "And your address?"

I gave him my address and he asked me to stay put while he ran my details through the police database via the terminal in his patrol car. When he returned, frown plastered on his face, it didn't take a behavioral analyst to work out there was trouble afoot.

"Do you have any ID on you?" he asked.

I ran my hands down my body and shook my head. "No, I don't. I guess I forgot to grab my purse when they were loading me into the hearse."

I chuckled.

He did not.

Ooookaaaaay.

"Is there a problem, Constable..." I squinted at his name badge. "Allan?"

"Senior Constable," he corrected.

Oh, FFS.

"Okay, is there a problem, *Senior* Constable?"

"Let's just say you're looking pretty good..." he said.

I smiled. Well, wasn't that nice? I figured I must have looked a fright, but nonetheless, he was kind enough to compliment—

"...for a corpse, that is," he added.

—me, especially after the crap week I'd had—wait, *what*? Did he just say *corpse*?

I blinked up at him. "I beg your pardon?"

"According to the system, Clarissa Josephine Hunt of Greville Street, Caroline Springs, is deceased."

"Well, I think we can safely say that I'm not," I said with another small chuckle. Senior Constable Allan, on the other hand, did not chuckle at all. Again.

Tough crowd.

I did my best to ignore the way he hadn't smiled or even so much as blinked throughout our entire conversation.

Who goes that long without blinking?

"I can explain," I said. "I had a little accident a few days ago, errant hockey puck, it's a long story. Anyway, I went to the hospital where I was declared dead, but obviously I wasn't because here I am. So, I guess they haven't updated their database or something?"

"Maybe," he said, studying me through narrowed eyes. "Maybe not."

"Excuse me?" I gawked.

"Well, here's the problem, you say you're Clarissa Hunt. My system says that Clarissa Hunt is dead."

"But I'm not dead."

"And if you could prove you actually *are* Clarissa Hunt there'd be no issue. But for now, you can see what kind of a pickle we're in, right?"

I scrubbed my face and tried not to panic.

This could not be happening to me. Seriously. In fact, I bet if I pinched myself right now, I'd wake up.

Ouch!

Nope. Definitely awake.

I gingerly rubbed the new sore spot on my arm, because I didn't quite have enough sore spots already, and fought back the tidal wave of tears threatening to roll down my face.

"Okay, let's try something different," Snr. Constable Allan said, clearly taking pity on me. "Why don't you tell me where you were at the time of the accident?"

I cleared my throat, acutely aware that my ass had started sweating.

For some ungodly reason, police officers really freaked me out. Despite never having been in trouble with the law in my life, I always felt like I was going to get arrested and locked up for the term of my natural life.

I'd watched *Prisoner*, *Wentworth* and *Orange is the New Black*. I knew what kind of life awaited me behind the gates of the Dame Phyllis Frost Detention Centre.

Ass-sweatingly terrifying.

This one time, I got pulled over by highway patrol near Ballarat and panicked so hard I ended up confessing to jaywalking, littering, and shoplifting a Snickers from our local milk bar when I was eleven. All the police officer wanted to do was advise me that my taillight was broken, and send me on my way.

Police especially freaked me out when they were questioning me about an accident that happened because I'd been murdered in an alleyway by a werewolf, come back to life in the back of a hearse, scared the testicles off some poor mortician, and caused an accident that closed a major freeway for three hours.

How in the hell was I going to explain any of that to someone when I didn't fully understand it, or fully believe it, myself?

Especially someone who could arrest me.

Or have me certified.

Or both.

Like I was saying, ass-sweat everywhere.

"So?" SC Allan said, interrupting my panic attack.

"What? Oh. I was, erm…in the back."

He looked up from his notebook, glanced at me, then at the hearse, then back at me. His brow rose. "What exactly do you mean 'in the back?'" he asked, pushing the peak of his cap back with the tip of his pen.

I thumbed toward the rear of the hearse. "I was, you know, in the back."

He sighed heavily. "Do I need to remind you, ma'am that it's illegal to travel unrestrained in the back of a vehicle—"

"Well, technically, I was restrained."

This time, SC Allan craned his head past me and squinted at the mangled hearse that was still nose-first in the embankment, rear end in the air, tailgate open, gurney akimbo, black body bag half in, half out.

"So, you're saying you were…" He pointed at the open body bag.

I nodded.

He studied me closely for a few seconds before a broad grin

split his face. "Oh, I get it. You and the mortician, you got something kinky going on. How does it work? You play dead and he pokes the—"

"Please, whatever you do, don't finish that sentence," I begged, feeling my cheeks heat. "Just, no. Who would even do something like that?"

He raised his brows. "You tell me. You're the one playing hide the salami in a coffin."

"I-I-I…" I stammered like Porky Pig for what felt like FOREVER and scrambled for a plausible explanation since the truth wasn't working so well. "I'll have you know there was no coffin."

Yep, because that was the important thing to clarify at that moment—not that I wasn't some deranged and, not to mention, sex-starved maven with a penchant for necrophilia games and light bondage. Nope. I felt compelled to clarify that I'd been in a body bag, and not a coffin. That's what was important

Idiot.

"And I wasn't playing hide the anything with anyone. I was in that hearse because I was… I was…"

Well, I couldn't exactly say dead, could I?

"You were in the back of the hearse because you were what?" SC Allan asked.

SO MUCH ASS-SWEAT!

He cocked a brow. "Well, you're obviously not dead. We've established that."

"Obviously," I said, forcing a laugh that was faker than my Aunt Mary's boob job and that was pretty fake given she was seventy-eight and her jumblies sat up around her hairy double chin like two firm, D-cup goiters.

I could feel the sweat trickling between my butt cheeks. Who the hell in the history of ever gets a nervous sweat in their *ass*?

"So," he said, pen still hovering over a blank page in his

notebook. "If you weren't dead, which we both agree on, then what were you doing in the back of the hearse?"

I looked at him hopefully, although exactly what I was hoping for, I couldn't tell you. That's when Senior Constable Allan slowly closed his notebook and pocketed it, along with his pen.

"How many cones have you had today, ma'am?" he asked.

"Cones? What, like ice cream?" I asked. Why the hell was he asking about ice cream? It was the middle of winter, for pity's sake.

"How about opiates or hallucinogens? Acid? MDMA? Maybe some codeine?" he continued.

"What? No. I don't do drugs," I replied. Then I understood. *Cones*. As in, bongs—marijuana.

"What about a history of mental illness? Psychotic breaks? Black outs?"

Ohmygod! He actually thought I was on drugs! Or crazy. Or on drugs *and* crazy!

I was so not crazy.

He was crazy for thinking I was crazy.

Crazy Senior Constable Allan.

"I'm not on drugs, and I have no history of mental illness, neither has anyone in my family. Well, actually, that's not entirely true, I guess you could say my Aunt Sandy is a bit strange. She's the one with the taxidermy fetish, stuffed Siamese cats mainly, and a collection of antique thimbles. She's bat-shit cra—"

SC Allan listened dutifully as I dug a hole deep enough to bury myself and the hearse in.

"Never mind," I said. "No one's crazy in my family."

SC Allan was trying hard not to lose his shit at me, but I could tell he was super frustrated. I could smell it—sweat, fresh-laid bitumen and burnt rubber. I just wasn't sure how successful his efforts to contain himself would be.

"Look, I can't help you unless you tell me the truth," he said in what I think was meant to be his good-cop voice. "So, why don't we start over? Can you tell me your name?"

"It's still Clarissa Josephine Hunt."

Senior Constable Allan pinched the bridge of his nose and took a long breath. "And I told you, Clarissa Josephine Hunt is dead. You can see it for yourself in the system."

"Well, if it's in the system then it must be true," I said, unable to shut my inner smartass up. "You know what, I think I am dead. What else could explain this bloody nightmare? I'm dead and I'm in hell, and this shit-show is my punishment for stealing the Snickers."

I may have been being slightly melodramatic.

"You know if you can't provide ID and I can't verify who you are, you can be arrested?"

"Arrested? But I'm telling you the truth!"

"And I'm just telling you that I can take you down to the station if you don't cooperate."

"But I *am* cooperating! My name is Clarissa Hunt and I live at—"

"Alrighty, have it your way," he said, unhooking a set of handcuffs from his utility belt and yanking my right arm behind my back. He snapped the first bracelet on. "Before continuing, I must inform you that you do not have to say or do anything, but anything you say or do can be given as evidence. Do you understand?"

"You're actually arresting me?" I asked as he snapped the second bracelet on. Not surprisingly, the steel was cold against my skin and pinched when he tightened the cuff.

"You have the right to communicate, or attempt to communicate, with a friend or relative to notify them of your whereabouts. You also have the right to communicate with, or attempt to communicate with, a legal practitioner."

"I don't have a legal pract—"

"If you are not a citizen of Australia, you have the right to communicate with, or attempt to communicate with, a representative of the consular office of which you are a citizen. Do you understand these rights as I have explained them to you? Do you wish to exercise any of these rights?"

"Listen, if you could just give me a ride home, then I could get you my ID. I have a license, passport, Medicare card... I think I've even got an old Blockbuster membership card somewhere."

"Do you wish to exercise any of these rights?"

"Oh, come on! I live like, twenty minutes from here."

"I look like an Uber to you?" SC Allan asked.

I sighed and dropped my head. "No."

"Then answer my question. Do you wish to exercise any of these rights?"

"No. I do not."

"Alright, then. Let's go."

TWO

BACK AT THE STATION, things did not get any better. The ass-sweating was reaching epic proportions—I could literally hear myself squelching as I walked—and it was pretty clear SC Allan thought I was some kind of kinky mental case.

Not that I blamed him.

"So, are you going to tell me your real name or not?" Senior Constable Allan asked, *again*. I swear, he was like a dog with a bone, this guy, and the more I repeated my name, the more annoyed he got, and I hadn't realized that was even possible.

I needed a change of strategy.

And fast.

Clearing my throat, I ran my tongue over my lips and batted my eyelids in a way I hoped didn't look like I was having a seizure. (Mental note: brush teeth when I get home.)

"Senior Constable Allan." I peered at his name badge again. "Gregory… Greg… May I call you Greg?"

"No," he replied without even blinking. What was with this guy and the not blinking? It was just plain weird.

"Right. Well then, it's obvious I'm not going to pull the wool over your eyes. You're far too clever for that."

He cocked a brow and eyed me warily.

"So, um, I'll come clean. When I was in the back of the hearse, I was actually—um, playing dead," I said.

"I see," Senior Constable Allan said. "So, you lied to me earlier?"

I fought the urge to pull my damp, wedgied panties out of my butt. I really had to see a doctor about that. This amount of ass sweat was *not* a normal reaction to, well...anything.

"Lie. It's such a harsh word," I said with a nervous laugh. "I was just, um, covering. You see, this is just a big misunderstanding; part of a little game we play, me and the mortician, that is. You know, for fun. Sexy fun," I wheezed, fanning myself. "I pretend to be dead and he..." I took a steadying breath. "Well, you know."

God, I hope he knew. I didn't want to have to explain it, especially as I had no idea what I was talking about.

"And the reason you ended up down the embankment?" he asked.

"Well, it's funny really."

Senior Constable Allan shifted in his seat. "Oh good, I could use a laugh."

This was sooooo not going well.

"I got a little claustrophobic," I said. "In the bag. You know how it is." I glanced up, only to be greeted by humorless hazel eyes. "Of course, you don't. Why would you? You're a normal person. Anyway, I freaked out and, um, screamed, and I guess it startled, er—"

I didn't know the driver's name.

I DIDN'T KNOW THE DRIVER'S NAME!

"Startled who?"

"My love-rrr."

Oh, God, kill me.

"Keith."

"Pardon?"

"Keith."

"Who the hell is Keith?"

"Your *love-rrr*. His name is Keith."

"Really?" I responded. "I mean, yes. Keith. That's his name."

Would it be wrong to slap myself in the face?

Senior Constable Allan frowned and shook his head. "And I'm supposed to believe—"

"Anyway, I'm not meant to talk when I'm in the back, because of all the deadness," I continued. "So, when I screamed, I guess I startled him or something and that's when he veered off the road and drove down the embankment?"

It wasn't meant to come out sounding like a question, and yet.

"I just didn't want to say anything earlier because, you know, embarrassing. Not for me, mind you. I'm fine with all the kink."

Dear God, please kill me. Again. Permanently, this time.

"But, for Kevin..."

"Keith."

"*Whatever*. He'd never admit to our liaisons. In fact, I bet if you asked him right now, he'd act like he had no idea what you were talking about. He'd probably deny all of it," I said. "Super clandestine, you know."

I tried to read SC Allan's expression, but he was giving nothing away. Who was this guy, fricken RoboCop or something?

What if he didn't believe me? What if he believed bloody Keith? Because, in Keith's defense, he was the one actually telling the truth, but he wasn't the one who was about to get committed to a mental institution.

I was FREAKING THE HELL OUT!

"He's married, you see—" I continued. (Great, now I was making the poor man out to be a pervert, a liar, *and* an adulterer.

I was definitely going to hell for this one.) "And his wife… She's away a lot because…she's a…um… She's a nun."

"A nun?" SC Allan's brows shot up.

"No. Not a nun, silly. She's a priest."

SOMEBODY STOP ME!

"You mean a minister? Like a reverend?"

"Sure. Why not? So, you know, no kink there—" I continued, rocking back and forth on the chair and willing the earth to open up and swallow me whole.

It didn't, of course.

What did happen, however, was a loud argument broke out in the hallway outside the interrogation room, mercifully halting the mortifying interrogation.

I could hear three voices, maybe four. I recognized two of them, Sonny and Vincent.

Ohhhh, magical.

Moments later, the interview room door swung open and a ruddy-faced police officer motioned for Senior Constable Allan to join him outside. Doing as he was told, SC Allan stood and left me on my own with my embarrassment and my sweaty butt.

There were more angry voices out in the hall, some protestations, and a lot of cuss words before the door swung open again and Sonny and Vincent stepped in.

"Clarissa, come along," Vincent said, taking me by the arm and helping me to my feet. "We've come to take you home."

I looked past Vincent to Senior Constable Allan. He was standing next to Sonny, who dwarfed him by at least five or six inches, and boy, he did not look amused. Sonny, on the other hand, looked as smug as a bug in a—no, that's not right. What did someone who was smug look like? They looked like Sonny, that's what.

"But, but…I haven't finished with the police, yet," I said, torn between fleeing with Sonny and Vincent, or staying put and seeing how this train wreck of an interview with SC Allan panned out.

Vincent looked at me disapprovingly. "Do you really want to stay here and have to explain everything to the officers?" he asked. "I'm sure they'd love to hear more about your kinky escapades."

I glared at him. "How did you even...? Were you *eavesdropping*?"

Vincent leaned forward and whispered in my ear, "I know everything, and if you keep going down this ridiculous path, I will need to facilitate your release from a mental institution rather than a local police station. So, come along before things get really ugly."

I did as Vincent asked and made my way to the door. Sonny, still with the shit-eating grin on his face, stepped aside to let me pass, but not before Senior Constable Allan blocked my exit.

"I don't know what's going on, or who any of you are, but this isn't over," he said. "I've got my eye on you, Miss Hunt."

"Ease up, cowboy," Sonny said, stepping between us and placing a massive hand on the center of the Senior Constable's chest. "Your work is done here."

"We'll see about that," SC Allan said, shrugging Sonny's hand off and turning away without so much as a second glance at any of us. "We'll see."

THREE

"WHAT WERE YOU THINKING?"

Vincent had been bellowing at me for nearly fifteen minutes without so much as stopping to take a breath. I was beginning to wonder if he actually breathed at all.

"Stop yelling," I said, bringing my hands up to cover my ears, purely for dramatic effect, of course. "You always talk to me like I'm a four-year-old."

Vincent hadn't taken the news that I'd "accidentally" told Nash about the possibility of my heart being illegally harvested from a werewolf all that well, as illustrated by the ranting.

He also seemed pretty peeved that I'd died...again.

Not to mention that I singlehandedly caused an accident that closed the M80 for three hours.

And gotten myself arrested.

"Perhaps if one were to stop acting like an infant, one would stop being treated like an infant," he said in a tone so clipped I thought I was at the dog groomers for a minute.

"If by *one* you mean me, then maybe *one* wouldn't act like *one* was an infant if the other *one* was the *one* who stopped treating *one* like *one* was an infant in the first place. *Capisce?*"

"I'm sure I don't."

"Just stop treating me like a kid, okay?" I huffed.

Vincent scrubbed his hands down his face. "I just don't understand what possessed you to tell a human, of all things, about something that's so utterly inconceivable to them. Why would you do that, pray tell?"

"Why do you think?" I didn't yell. I only raised my voice. It was a demi-yell, at best. "I was desperate. It's clear that you lot have no idea what's going on, so I figured Nash might have access to information that could help."

"And did he?" Vincent asked.

"Not exactly."

"Kindly elaborate."

"What if I don't want to?"

"It wasn't a request, Clarissa," he said through clenched teeth.

Bossy bastard.

"Fine. I asked him to show me my medical history, you know, so I could see if it contained any information about my heart donor."

Vincent's expression softened. "Go on," he said with the hint of a nod.

"But it turns out my history hasn't been uploaded to their computer system yet."

"Convenient."

"Right? That's what I thought. So, I convinced Nash to take me to the records room to see if we could find the hard copy."

"And exactly how did you convince him to do that?" Sonny asked.

I eyed him, noting his tense jaw and defensive body language. "I can be very persuasive if I want to be."

"I bet," he grumbled.

Was I sensing a little jealousy? Interesting.

"Of course, if I'd known it was going to be in the basement, I might have thought twice about going, but I didn't. So, we're down in the record room and the strangest thing happened. I got a really weird feeling."

"What kind of feeling?" Vincent asked.

"I guess you could describe it as foreboding, maybe? Like a premonition." I shrugged. "Anyway, we were heading back to Nash's office when the werewolves spotted us, and I guess you know the rest."

Vincent shook his head. "So, you're telling me you risked everything, your life, Nash's life, the integrity of this organization and the secrets we've successfully hidden from the human race for *over two thousand years*, all for nothing?"

"Well, when you put it like that."

"How did they even know you'd be there, that's what I'd like to know?" Sonny asked.

"Who?"

"The werewolves," he replied.

"Where?"

He sighed. "At the clinic. How did the werewolves know you were going to be there?"

"Beats me," I said. "How did *you* find out where I was?"

Vincent and Sonny glanced at each other, and my spidey-senses were tingling. Something fishy was going on.

"Well?" I continued. "I'm waiting."

"We monitor police radio frequencies. We learned you had been arrested and were being interviewed by authorities. So, we intervened."

I narrowed my eyes at them. "How very convenient."

I didn't like convenient explanations. They usually ended up being contrived and not at all convenient.

"By the way, I'm going to go out on a limb and suggest you might have a double agent in your midst."

"Impossible," Vincent barked.

"Really?"

"Everyone who serves the Patrons is carefully vetted."

"Not me," I replied.

"You don't exactly serve us, do you?" Sonny said.

"Well, I—"

"You're more like a diva, swanning in here with your stunts and attitude." Vincent threw his hands in the air, maybe for dramatic effect, maybe from frustration, it was hard to tell. "I should have listened to Sonny," he said, pacing back and forth behind his gigantic desk. "I should have known he'd be right about you."

"What's that supposed to mean? Right about *what* about me?" I turned to Sonny. "What exactly did you say?"

"Sorry." He shrugged. "Confidential."

"Yeah, I bet." Confidential, my ass. "Anyway, I wouldn't say it was a complete bust. At least now I know where they keep the hard copy files."

"Which, you will never attempt to retrieve yourself," Vincent said.

"Why not?"

"If I need to explain why to you, then I seriously underestimated your intelligence."

I chose to ignore him. "Plus, I bet Nash totally believes in werewolves now." I grinned. "And he's a smart guy. It might be handy to have him on our side."

Sonny snort-laughed.

He so *was* jealous!

"Nash is laying in the ICU at the Royal Melbourne Hospital with catastrophic injuries," Vincent snapped. "He's clinging to life by the barest of threads. He'll be lucky to come out of this without losing most of his internal organs, assuming he wakes up at all which, from what I understand, is highly unlikely."

"Oh, I—"

"And if he does recover, and that's a big *if*, I'm not entirely sure he'll remember his own name, much less become a werewolf rights advocate."

"Do you always have to be such a Negative Nancy?" I huffed.

"Seems you bring out that side of me," Vincent replied.

"Well, can I go see him?" I asked.

"No," Sonny snapped.

"Why not?"

"Because I said."

"Oh, well, that's a good reason."

"Why would you want to see him, anyway? Don't you think you've caused him enough damage?"

I sneered at Sonny. "Maybe I could help him."

"How exactly?" Vincent asked.

"I could keep him company."

"What part of clinging to life by the barest of threads did you not understand?" Sonny asked.

I shot him the stink-eye. "Maybe I could bring him soup?"

"Great idea," Sonny said. "Right now, most of his insides are on the outside, and he's shitting into a teeny plastic bag, but I'm sure some of your chicken noodle will fix all that right up."

"You don't have to be such a douche about it," I grumbled.

'I'm serious, Clarissa," Vincent said. "I don't want you going anywhere near Nash. No visiting. No calling to get status updates. Zero contact until I can repair the damage you've caused him and this organization."

"*Fiiiiine*! You don't have to keep harping on about it," I said, rolling my eyes.

"And you are absolutely not, under any circumstances, to attempt to retrieve your file from the Myer Clinic. *Capisce?*"

"Yes. I get it. I'm not slow," I said

"Hm," he grunted before he and Sonny marched out of his office.

FOUR

I THINK WE ALL KNOW the first thing I did when I left Vincent's office was head to the hospital to see if I could get an update on Nash's condition. His situation was my fault, after all, and I couldn't just abandon him in his time of need, could I?

On arriving, I totally expected to be told that I couldn't see Nash because I wasn't family. I was also expecting they'd refuse to give me an update on his condition because, again, not family. I also expected to be able to use my wily charms to circumvent their *family only* policy and coerce some kind of information from whichever unsuspecting nightshift nurse I came across.

What I wasn't expecting, however, was to be told Nash was no longer a patient at Royal Melbourne Hospital.

"What does that even mean? Is he *dead*?" I gasped, my hand immediately reaching for the top of my scar.

"Dr. Nash is no longer a patient at this hospital," the very pleasant receptionist sitting behind the information desk repeated, complete with fake smile stretched tightly across his face. I wanted to slap that smile into next week but restrained myself.

"So, he's *not* dead?" I asked, searching for some small reassurance from Mr. Plastic Fantastic in scrubs.

"Dr. Nash is no longer a patient—"

"Yes, yes, I heard you the first three times. He's no longer a patient in this hospital, *blah, blah, blah.* But it's not like I'm asking you to—"

"Is there anything else I can help you with?" he said, fake smile never faltering.

"Look, all I want to know is if Nash has been discharged? Or transferred to another hospital? Or has he—" I noticed the receptionist's eyes flicker over my shoulder, so I turned to see two burly security guards making their way toward the information desk. "Oh, come on," I groaned. "Security? Really? Am I *that* scary?"

The receptionist continued to smile at me like some maniacal Cheshire cat, and I expended what little was left of my self-control not to punch him right in his rhinoplastied schnoz.

I rolled my eyes. "Fine, be a jerk," I said, scurrying toward the exit before the two guards had the chance to cuff me or sling me out into the street like in those old westerns my dad would watch on a Saturday night. I'd been roughed up and arrested one too many times. I'd reached my humiliation quota.

I stood in the dimly lit car park for I don't know how long, trying to decide what to do next. I could sneak down to the morgue and see if Nash was there. That would at least answer the *is he dead or alive* question. But given the week I'd had, there was a good chance some overzealous orderly would remember me from the hockey puck incident, refuse to believe I wasn't dead, and stuff me back into a body bag.

No thank you.

I could go to the Myer Clinic. Maybe he'd been transferred there to continue specialized care? I looked at my watch. It was late and I didn't want a repeat of what'd just happened, so that was off the table until morning.

I could go to his house, break in and see if he was there. Only I didn't know where he lived, not that that was much of a problem. It wasn't that hard to get someone's address if you knew where to look. But if I did that, someone might see me and call the police, and then I'd get arrested for trespassing or impersonating a living person again. As pleasant as SC Allan seemed— not—I didn't fancy having to explain myself out of a second weird-ass, supernatural situation for the evening. Especially since I'd done such a shitty job of it the first time.

I was debating whether or not to go back to see Vincent, when I noticed the two security guards still watching me from the hospital lobby.

I scowled at them both and flipped them the bird before trudging to my car, deciding the best place for me was home. I was tired, and hungry, and in desperate need of a shower.

Finding Nash would just have to wait until morning, because at that moment, all I wanted was to wash the day's unpleasantness off me, and crawl into bed.

FIVE

I STOOD IN THE SHOWER until the water ran cold and my skin was all pruney. The steam had eased some of the stiffness from my limbs, and the familiar scent of my grapefruit and lemongrass body wash soothed my aching bones and eased my troubled mind.

The more I thought about what had been happening, the more freaked out I was getting; and the more freaked out I was getting, the more desperate I was to get to the bottom of it all, so I could return to my normal life, if that was even possible.

Wrapping myself in a fluffy towel, one of the gorgeous Mark Tuckey organic cotton ones I'd ordered from Adairs during lockdown, I stepped out of the shower, and padded over to the vanity. It was a slick, wall-mounted unit flanked by matching hand-blown, Murano glass chandeliers, and topped with an antique Baroque mirror I found on eBay. It had a thick, hand-carved frame that had been painted in white chalk paint, and at $275, was an absolute bargain—especially compared to the price of the Murano chandeliers.

I swiped at the condensation on the mirror, peered closely at my reflection and frowned. For someone who'd died three times in a matter of days, I looked pretty damn healthy.

My cheeks were rosy; my eyes were clear. Hell, I'd even go so far as to say they seemed greener than their usual hazel, which was impossible without my colored contacts, which I knew I wasn't wearing because they were sitting in their plastic container right there on the vanity next to my toothbrush and night serum.

The bluish bruise across my forehead, the one I'd gotten courtesy of the werewolf in the alley, had faded, and the skin on my body was smooth and pink, showing hardly any sign of having been mauled by said werewolf.

I didn't even have any bags under my eyes, which was a pleasant change. If I hadn't known better, I would have thought I'd spent the afternoon at Dr. Murphy's surgery—he's my derma- tologist—getting a cheeky Botox treatment and a quick dermabrasion, and not being savaged in an alley, or falling out the back of a hearse at high speed.

Truth be told, I was beginning to doubt I'd actually died at all. Maybe Nash had been right? Maybe none of it was true? Maybe when I'd been clipped by the hockey puck, I'd simply sustained a concussion? And maybe I'd fallen off the balcony all by myself. It wasn't outside the realm of possibility. I wasn't exactly known for my grace and agility. Maybe I just had some kind of acquired brain injury? Maybe this whole saga had all just been a bad dream and I'd wake up any minute, and realize all of it had been a figment of my imagination.

And maybe I was just clutching at straws, looking for ways to explain away all the weirdness that had been happening to me and I had, indeed, gone completely insane?

Or maybe I was just hungry?

I dressed in my comfiest sweatpants and favorite Oodie, the one with Jack Skellington all over it, and wandered downstairs so I could fix myself a snack. I couldn't remember the last time I'd eaten and I was about ready to chew my own arm off from starvation.

As I reached the bottom landing, Miss Miranda shot past me, heading upstairs and presumably to bed. She liked to pick and choose which side she slept on, based on…well, I didn't know what she based her decisions on. Kitty whim, I liked to call it.

She'd been less than happy to see me when I slid into the house via the access door that connected the garage to the laundry. Seems she'd grown accustomed to Sonny taking care of her in my absence, and it was quite clear she was less than pleased to see me arrive instead of her new bestie who lavished her with pats and cuddles. Not that I blamed her. I wouldn't mind some pats and cuddles from Sonny. Lucky fluffy wench.

As I sidestepped, so I could avoid trampling my furry flat mate, I noticed light streaming from under the kitchen door, and paused. I couldn't remember leaving the light on. In fact, I was one hundred percent certain I hadn't so much as set foot in the kitchen before I went upstairs. Now, the light was on, which could only mean one of two things:

1. I'd left it on *before* the puck incident, so my next electricity bill was going to resemble the national debt of all the countries in Eastern Europe. Yippee.
2. Or I had another bloody intruder in my house.

I wasn't sure which option I preferred, but if it was an intruder, I'd be damned if I was going to let this one get away scot free.

Glancing around, I picked up the only thing I could find that might vaguely serve as a weapon—an old umbrella that had turned inside out and ripped in three spots during that freak storm last summer; the one with the hailstones the size of cricket balls.

Anyway, the brolly was of no use anymore, and yet I'd kept it, so I gave myself an internal high-five for having been too lazy to throw it out.

I briefly considered using my handbag to beat the intruder to death—God knew it was heavy enough to cause a fatal wound. Somehow, though, the umbrella seemed more practical. I might not be able to knock the bastard out with it, but I could leave a nasty hole in his pancreas if I could get close enough to stab him without being eviscerated first.

I crept closer to the door and could hear movement in the kitchen. Drawers being opened and closed, plates and cutlery clattering, glasses clinking, the fridge opening and closing, jars open—*wait*. Was my intruder making a *snack*? Seriously? It was one thing to break and enter with intent to cause grievous bodily harm; it was quite another to raid my pantry and help yourself to all my scrummy-yummy goodies. Well, someone was about to get smacked down. Hard.

Mustering all the (very little) energy I had left, I kicked the kitchen door open and charged in, swinging the brolly like a broadsword, and screeching like a dementor.

There was another scream, a far more masculine one, followed by the sound of smashing glass.

"Jesus!" the intruder said, raising his hands to the side. "Clarissa! Stop! It's me."

I stopped yelling, squinted at the man standing at my kitchen bench with a slice of buttered bread in one hand and a shattered jar of Vegemite at his feet, and lowered the umbrella.

"*Nash?*" I said, feeling a sense of relief wash over me. "What the hell are you doing here?"

"Waiting for you...and getting the jellybeans scared out of me," he replied.

I eyed the margarine container and cheese slices laying open on the kitchen bench.

"And making a snack," he added with a shrug. "Can I put my

arms down or are you going to jab me with that thing?" he asked, jutting his stubbled chin at my mangled umbrella, which had sprung open in all the screeching and swinging, and was now hanging limply by my side like a mauled squid.

I nodded and dropped the umbrella. "You can put them down," I said.

"Thank you. Have you got a dustpan? I made a bit of a mess."

"Sure." I padded across the kitchen and into the laundry where I kept my cleaning stuff, stepping around the shards of broken glass and globs of black yeast spread splattered all over the floor.

When I returned, Nash had picked up most of the glass and was dutifully wrapping it in paper towel. What was it with hot men picking up shattered glass in my kitchen? Was it like a new TikTok thing? Because if it was, it was waaaaay better than watching Gen Xers awkwardly lip sync to hip hop songs they wouldn't otherwise be caught dead listening to.

"Sorry for scaring you," Nash said, rising to his full height. "I waited outside for like an hour and when you didn't come home, I decided—"

"To help yourself to my snacks?" I asked.

"No, actually, I helped myself to your toilet. The snacks were an afterthought."

I took a seat at my kitchen table and leaned back in the chair. "What are you even doing here? And how did you get in?"

"I found your spare key under the fake rock in your garden bed."

I really had to up my home security game. People were getting into my house easier than my Cousin Stacey's knickers which, PS, wasn't that hard providing you had a penis and a heartbeat.

And no, I wasn't slut-shaming. I was just stating the facts.

"And I'm here because I was worried about you," he said,

putting the bread, margarine, and cheese back where he'd found them. "You weren't exactly doing well the last time I saw you."

"*I* wasn't doing well?" I scoffed, pointing at myself. "What about *you*?"

"What about me?"

"Um, your injuries. I wasn't the one that was carted off in an ambulance and admitted straight to ICU because I was hanging on to life by the barest of threads."

I neglected to mention the part where I was shredded by a lycan, died, fell out the back of the hearse and got arrested. There were only so many times I wanted to relive that humiliation.

"Neither was I," he replied.

"Oh, come on, I saw your injuries. They told me, in no uncertain words, that you wouldn't survive."

"Who told you? The hospital?"

"And now here you are, in my kitchen and looking good... so, so good, err...for someone who was knock, knock, knocking on heaven's door just a couple of days ago, that is. Which raises the question, why aren't you knock, knock, knocking anymore?"

"Clarissa, look," Nash said, leaning casually on the bench. "I don't know who you spoke to or why they told you any of that because it's just not true. You can see for yourself, I'm okay." He stretched his arms out to the sides and turned in a slow circle.

He was doing more than okay, he was doing fiiiine. He had that sexy semi-beard thing going on, which was just divine. He wore faded blue jeans, a Pearl Jam t-shirt that really hugged his nicely muscled frame (he *definitely* worked out) and black hiking boots. He had a rugged, but refined look about him; kind of 90s cool but without the flannel.

Most important, he looked perfectly healthy and not at all like he'd been anywhere near death. "But they told me you were dying. I saw your injuries. You were gutted like a fish."

"Who told you?" Nash asked. "Because I don't know what to

say. I mean, I got some nasty contusions, I'm moving like an eighty- year-old, and I've got more stitches than a Country Women's Association quilt exhibition, but nothing life threatening. And I definitely wasn't in ICU."

I felt myself frown, then huffed out an exasperated breath. "I am so stupid," I grumbled. "You'd think I'd have learned not to trust them by now, wouldn't you? I mean, every single thing they've ever told me has turned out to be bullshit and let's face it, their whole *raison d'être* is shady AF—"

"Who's shady?" Nash asked.

"And they're so bloody convincing. That's the thing, isn't it? They make it all sound soooooo plausible."

"*Who?*"

"Huh?"

"Who makes what sound so plausible?"

"The Patrons."

"Patrons?"

"You know, the Patrons of—" I slapped my hand over my mouth and squeaked at my sheer stupidity.

Nash didn't know anything about the Patrons.

Nash didn't know anything about the fricken Patrons!

And I was pretty sure Vincent wanted to keep it that way, especially after the fifteen-minute bollocking I'd gotten for simply mentioning the vague possibility that I *might* have told Nash that my donor heart *may*, or *may not*, have come from a werewolf.

Vincent was going to forever kill me this time, for sure.

"Erm."

"The Patrons of *Erm*?"

I chuckled. "Hehe. Sorry, I smacked my head pretty hard in the alley." I tapped my index finger against my temple. "Still not functioning quite right."

Nash raised his brows and pinned me with his incredible gaze. Who was I kidding? There was no point in lying to Nash, not now; not after I'd nearly gotten him killed. I simply had to tell him everything.

Vincent was going to throw a shit fit, either way. He was going to lock me up in the dungeon of doom, with no Wi-Fi and no manicures. I needed someone, a human someone, to know what was going on, so they could alert the authorities if something went horribly wrong. More horribly wrong than it already had, that is.

Like it or not, Nash was involved now, and he had as much right to know as I had.

So I spilled my guts, and told him everything. I told him about Vincent, about Sonny, about the Patrons and their subterranean cathedral. I told him about Azrael, my heart transplant—everything. I told him every single detail I'd had the misfortune of learning myself.

By the end of it, I felt like I needed a nap and a massage. "I know it sounds farfetched," I said, but Nash simply chuckled.

"Listen, I'm hangry. I'm tired, I'm sore, and I've been showering six times a day trying to wash the smell of alley off me. After what I've seen in the past few days, nothing and I do mean *nothing*, surprises me."

Hm. I was sure I could come up with a few more tasty morsels that'd tip him over the edge, but thought better of it.

"So, why me?" he asked.

"What do you mean?"

"Why reach out to me? Why not push these Patron folk for more information?"

"They're no help. They talk in circles and lie more than Charles Ponzi. I just wanted to talk to someone who wasn't a giant supernatural freak. But, as it turns out, you were as clueless as I was."

"Sorry about that," he said.

I shook my head. "No need to apologize. It was always going to be a long shot."

This whole, shitty situation was a long shot. Nothing seemed to be going smoothly. The more I learned, the less I understood, and the less I understood, the more frustrated I got.

"So, all that stuff about dying and coming back to life, the werewolf heart transplant...you were completely serious?"

I nodded. "Yep."

Nash rubbed his face vigorously, before running both hands through his lush hair. "How is any of this even possible?" he said. "I mean, werewolves? In inner city Melbourne? It's just—"

"Mind-boggling?"

"I was going to say ludicrous, but even that feels like an understatement."

"I hear you. When I first learned about all this paranormal stuff—"

"Which was when, exactly?"

I looked up and to the right. "Um, like two weeks ago." I sighed. "God, has it only been a fortnight? It feels like a hundred years."

"So all this isn't common knowledge, then? I'm not just out of the supernatural loop, or something?"

"God, no. Most people don't know jack-shit about the Inner World."

"Inner World?"

"Yeah, it's what the Patrons call the paranormal stuff. Something about wearing masks and not wanting to show people their faces or something. I don't know. I'd tuned out by that stage of the conversation."

I slumped forward and rested my elbows on the table. "Two weeks ago, I was just like you, blissfully unaware of any of this insanity. But then I died, came back to life, got mauled by werewolves, flung off a balcony, died again and discovered there are people—persnickety, disagreeable people—who have made it their life's work to hide all this stuff from we poor, unsuspecting humans."

"And *they* would be the Patrons? The persnickety ones, I mean."

I nodded. "That's them. Just, whatever you do, don't mention any of this to anyone, okay?"

Nash laughed. "You're kidding, right? I'm a doctor. They'd lock me up and throw away my medical license if I told anyone this crazy story."

"Just promise to keep it on the down low," I said, tapping the side of my nose. "Strictly confidential, because if you don't, the Patrons will likely kill you and you won't have to worry about having anything revoked."

"Scout's honor," Nash said, holding up the three middle fingers of his right hand. "I won't tell a soul."

"You were a Scout?"

"Does that surprise you?"

"No. You totally strike me as a good-deed-for-the-day kinda guy."

He smiled, which showed off his perfect dimples, and shot me a cheeky wink. "So, these Patron guys are basically Men in Black but for monsters?"

"No, of course not. It's nothing like that." I paused and considered his statement. "Actually, it's *exactly* like that," I corrected. "Only, they aren't half as amusing. I'll introduce you one day."

"I can hardly wait," Nash said, joining me at the table.

"But be warned, they're extremely testy."

"I'm getting that impression," he said.

We sat in silence for a few moments.

"So, what do we do now?" he asked.

"Well, since you were no help to me... No offense."

"None taken."

"I guess we'll have to do this the old-fashioned way."

Nash's face lit up. "We gonna go and rough up some snitch-es?" he said with a little too much vim. "Are we going to tie someone to a chair and kneecap them? Or crush their head in a vise until they spill the beans?"

"Ease up, *paesan*," I said, pulling my laptop out of its carry bag, flipping it open and firing it up. "There will be no roughing up of anything, including the beans."

"Sorry," he said, sheepishly.

"I'm beginning to think you and the Patrons would get along very well," I said.

"I clearly spent too much time watching *The Sopranos*."

"I'll have to take your word for it."

"You've never seen it?"

I shook my head.

"Let me guess, you're a *MAFS* kinda gal? *Below Deck*, maybe?"

"No, I'm a YouTube kinda *woman*. No reality for me."

"None whatsoever? Not even *Selling Houses Australia*?" Nash asked.

I paused. "Fine. I do watch *Selling Houses*, and *Farmer Wants a Wife*, but if you tell another soul, I will reach down your throat, grab hold of your small intestine and turn you inside out," I said whilst simultaneously tapping on the keyboard.

"You paint quite the word picture, don't you?" he said, and smiled at me.

My fingers flew across the keys and in no time, I'd opened three browsers, six online chats, a dozen or so blogs, *and* the Vatican archives (the private ones, not the public site everyone else has access to).

As always, the online world was alive and buzzing with virtual chitter-chatter, and watching the conversations scroll up the screen filled me with a familiar sense of calm. This was my world. This is where I felt happy and in control. This was my tribe.

"I should have done this days ago," I muttered, peering at the new discussions popping up online, clicking a few chats, and opening blogs.

"Where'd you learn to do that?"

"Do what?" I kept my eye on the screen.

Nash pointed to the laptop. "That."

"Why?"

"I beg your pardon?" he asked.

"Why do you want to know?"

"I guess, well, I'm just curious. You're the only influencer I've ever met."

I glanced up at him. "What makes you think I'm an influencer?" I asked.

Nash dropped his gaze and fidgeted with his fingernails.

"Have you been online stalking me, Dr. Nash?" I smiled.

"I think stalking is an exaggeration," he replied. "But I may have done some research. I make a point of finding out as much as I can about anyone I get involved with."

"Oh?"

His face turned the sweetest shade of pink.

"Professionally speaking, of course," he qualified.

"Of course." I nodded, trying not to stare at his cheeks.

The ensuing silence wasn't at all awkward.

"Anyway, I'm not an influencer. I'm a digital content creator," I clarified. "My clients are the influencers. And for your information, I work really hard," I said, refocusing on the computer screen.

"I never said you didn't."

"Just because I don't have some snooze-worthy, nine-to-five job with twelve percent superannuation and four weeks paid leave per year, doesn't mean mine isn't a perfectly legitimate career."

"Okay."

"What would you prefer I did? Become a lawyer like that slime ball, Ziggy?"

"Who's Ziggy?"

"Or a used car salesperson? Maybe I should just marry some old, rich schmuck with season tickets to the ballet and a swollen prostate, and leech off him until he kicks it—"

Nash held his hands up. "Um, so I'm not sure what's going on, but I think we may have hit a nerve somewhere back there."

I sighed and shook my head. "I'm sorry. Questions about my career should come with a trigger warning," I said. "I've grown so accustomed to either being mocked or criticized about what I do for a living, I tend to get a little defensive when people ask about it. That's on me."

"People genuinely give you a hard time?"

"You wouldn't believe."

"I've never experienced anything like that," he said.

"You're a thoracic surgeon. Who the hell is going to give you grief about that?"

"My parents, for one," he said, grimly. "They expected me to follow in the family business."

"And what business is that?"

"Used car sales and marrying rich old men dying of prostate cancer," he said with a heart-fluttering grin.

I smiled, thankful for the welcomed comedic relief. I liked that he could make me laugh in the face of all the weirdness. I liked that he was so clearly a caring human being who didn't jump to judge others — actually, I was just glad he was a human being full stop. I liked the way his blue eyes sparkled when he blushed, and I liked that he wasn't trying to convince me I was some kind of supernatural weirdo. It was such a pleasant change.

"In my experience, people have a tendency to devalue what they don't understand," Nash said in a beautifully lyrical, soothing tone. "It's easier to trash something new or different than it is to open your mind and take the time to learn about it."

"Spot on," I said, enjoying the easy conversation we'd fallen into. "Joke's on them, though. While they're sitting on the toilet, trolling TikTok for pantry restock videos, my clients are rolling in the green."

"Rolling in the green? Are you sure you've never watched *The Sopranos*?"

"Very," I replied.

Nash watched as I tapped away on the keyboard.

"Mind if I get something to drink?"

"Help yourself," I said, pointing to the fridge.

He stood and walked back into the kitchen, affording me a clear view of his denim-clad butt. Nice.

"Want anything?" he asked.

"You have no idea," I muttered.

"Sorry?"

Damn I hate it when my internal monologue isn't so internal.

"Nothing, thank you," I replied, super-casually, of course.

I watched as he cracked open a Corona before tossing the cap in the recycling bin and taking a long swig. Who knew a bobbing Adam's apple could be so hypnotic? I gave myself a mental shake and turned back to the keyboard.

"So, just let me get this straight," he said, returning to the table. "You record a couple of TikToks of your client putting on makeup or whatever, slap some snappy hashtags into the comments, and boom! The video goes viral and you earn yourself a nifty commission. Am I warm?"

I stopped typing and stared up at him. "Don't be so obtuse, Steven," I said. His good-natured teasing put me at ease and I found myself wondering if it was unethical to have a teeny-weeny crush on someone who worked for a guy who once had their hands in your chest? There wasn't anything about that in the Hippocratic Oath was there? *Thou shalt not allow thy mentor's patients covet thee.* Or was it like a gray area?

"Then explain it to me, please," he said, propping his perfect body on the kitchen table. "No teasing or mocking, I promise. I genuinely want to understand." Nash traced an X on his impressive chest.

I smiled. Part of me wanted to believe him, and part of me was still skeptical. He seemed like he was telling the truth. But if I'd learned one thing over the past few days, it was that the truth could be quite subjective.

"Oh, come on. Tell me." Nash swatted at me playfully and I delighted in how warm and safe he'd managed to make me feel, despite the somewhat chaotic start we'd had to the evening. It was the first time I'd felt so at ease in what felt like forever, and I hadn't realized just how much I'd missed it. "So, how did you choose this as a career?"

"Actually, it kinda chose me."

Nash looked puzzled. "How's that?"

"Well, before Poppy died, we posted a bunch of videos to YouTube, you know, talking about our experiences, educating people about dilated cardiomyopathy, the importance of becoming an organ donor...that kind of stuff. The videos got a fair bit of traction, and we were building quite a following, but then Poppy died." I must have looked grief-stricken because Nash reached over and covered my hand with his. It was a kind gesture, comforting, warm. It made me feel safe.

"The one I eventually posted about her death went viral, then so did another, and another. Everyone was so supportive and kind. It was wonderful. I didn't have many friends of my own. Being terminally ill doesn't exactly lend itself to building life-long friendships, or any really. So it was a nice, safe way to meet new people."

Nash took another pull on his beer and nodded. I noted he hadn't removed his hand from mine yet, like it was perfectly natural for it to be there.

"Then, after my transplant, I posted about my recovery and some of the mental issues I was dealing with."

"And you felt comfortable sharing all this with the whole

world?" he asked, a look of surprise spreading across his handsome features. "Something so personal, I mean."

"Sure," I said, breaking eye contact. "A lot goes on in the old noggin when you're an organ recipient." I tapped the side of my head. "You need to get it out of here, otherwise, it'll make you nuts."

"Which issues did you talk about most?"

I sighed. This was not something I typically liked to talk about. It was too heavy. Too painful. Just, too much.

"I'm really interested," Nash said, as if sensing my reluctance to discuss it. "After surgery, I don't get many chances to explore this kind of thing with patients. It's mostly about getting medications right and monitoring for rejection and infection. I'd appreciate the opportunity to learn more about the other side of things, if you don't mind, of course."

Oh, I minded. I minded a lot. But I also knew that one of the best ways to recover from any type of trauma was to talk about it with people you trust. The real question was, could I trust Nash?

I decided there was only one way to find out.

"Firstly," I said, throwing caution to the wind and giving him the benefit of the doubt. "I was dealing with grief. I mean, losing a sibling is one thing, but losing your twin to a disease you've also got..."

Nash shook his head. "I'm an only child, so I can't even begin to imagine."

"Be thankful you can't," I said, absently reaching for the top of my transplant scar.

"Does it bother you?" Nash asked, pointing at the now-healed wound his mentor had created.

"My scar?"

Nash nodded.

"It doesn't hurt anymore, if that's what you mean."

"You touch it a lot."

"It's a habit, I guess."

"Are you embarrassed by it?"

"Not at all. I just...you could say I hate it. It's like a foot-long, daily reminder about my transplant."

"And being reminded that you received life-saving surgery is a bad thing?" he said with a frown.

Was that shock? Sarcasm? Incredulity? I got it. Believe me. How could anyone process what I'd been through unless they'd experienced it for themselves? Or at least had someone to explain it to them.

"Being reminded that someone had to die just so you could live is surprisingly difficult to accept," I replied.

Nash's brows shot up.

"I know, right? My therapist had a field day with that little nugget," I continued. "Survivor's guilt, they call it. Took me seven-years and $50,000 of Daddy's hard-earned cash to learn to say that without bursting into tears and retreating into my dark place." I sighed. "Of course, I'm over all that now. Mostly."

There was another prolonged silence, but this one wasn't awkward. This time, Nash was just taking the time to process.

I was cool with that.

"I must admit, I've never understood it—I mean..." Nash seemed flustered and confused. "I always assumed organ recipients would be ecstatic, or at a minimum, relieved after their transplant surgery. You know, celebrating having the chance to live. It never crossed my mind that it wouldn't be all happy, happy, joy, joy."

"It's not that I'm not grateful or happy," I said. "Because I absolutely am. How could I not be when somebody—a complete stranger and their kindhearted family—gave me the ultimate gift? But I just couldn't help feeling there was something wrong about the whole thing. Plus I kept wondering who my donor was; what kind of person they were. That kind of thing."

"They were a werewolf apparently," he said.

"Right." I smiled. "But I didn't know that at the time. No, I wanted to know what their favorite food was. What types of music they listened to. Would I suddenly gorge hot dogs and blast Eminem if that's what they did?"

"It doesn't work that way, Clarissa, Organs don't have memories."

"Don't they?"

"Well," he said, finally removing his hand from mine and rubbing the back of his neck. "Organ memory is not an unheard-of phenomenon. Many reputable researchers believe it's possible for donor organs to hold and even pass on the characteristics and experiences of its original owner onto the new one. It's known as cellular memory."

"I know." I replied with a shrug.

"But it's rare and unproven."

"But it does happen?"

Nash sighed. "Theoretically, yes."

"So, not so stupid, then?"

"I never said you were stupid."

I looked into his clear, blue eyes. "Not in so many words."

He lowered his gaze. "I'm sorry."

"That's okay. Now, where was I?"

"Cellular memory."

"Right. Okay, there was that, but I also kept wondering, why me? Why me and not Poppy? Why couldn't Dr. Chaney save us both?"

"Well, I can actually explain that." Nash jumped straight into doctor mode. "There are a number of factors that affect—"

I held my hand up. "You don't have to give me the pep talk, Doc," I reassured him. "It was a rhetorical question. I know how the process works, and like I told you, I'm better now. Mostly."

Nash didn't continue his line of questioning, for which I was truly grateful. Instead we sat quietly for a few minutes, lost in our own thoughts.

"That got dark pretty quickly, didn't it?" Nash asked, eventually.

"Yep." I nodded.

"We done with it now?"

"Definitely."

"Good. You were saying?"

"I was telling you about how I got into this line of work."

"Then please continue," Nash said, and I was relieved.

"That's pretty much it. I developed a bit of a cult following, took digital comms and marketing at uni, managed to land some C-and B-list clients to begin with," I said with a shrug. "The rest, as they say, is history."

"You know, I'm very impressed by the way you've turned what was effectively a hobby into a successful business empire," he said, smiling at me. "That's a pretty big achievement, especially for someone so young and who's experienced the health problems you have. You're quite the entrepreneur."

His eyes were warm and his tone soft and he smelled like freshly cut grass and lemonade. It was quite the heady combination.

"It's not exactly cardiothoracics," I said, willing myself not to get too swept away in what was probably just his well-honed bedside manner. I had more important things to deal with. Like...um...stuff...and things...and...never mind. "I'm not saving lives over here."

"You don't know that," Nash said. "You don't know what impact your words or videos have had on some other kid who thought they were going to die. And who knows how much awareness you've raised about DCM? A shit ton, I'm betting. You probably saved more people than you could even begin to imagine."

I felt my cheeks flush and a delightful warmth rush through my body. This guy was either legitimately amazing and sweet and wonderful, or that was the best performance I'd seen since Sean Penn in *Dead Man Walking*.

"Plus, I can think of at least one life you've saved. I doubt I'd be in the shape I'm in today if it weren't for you."

"Well, when you put it that way—"

Right then, the kitchen filled with plumes of purple and silver smoke, accompanied by the familiar smell of Allen's jelly lollies and fresh peaches. Moments later, Sonny materialized in a *poof* of sparkling glitter.

SONOFABITCH!

Nash sprang out of his chair like a high school kid caught cheating on a pop quiz, and I found myself pushing back on mine, as I swatted at the smoke tendrils that swirled and wafted around us.

"What the hell, Sonny?" I grumbled. "Ever heard of knocking?"

He ignored my question, instead inserting himself between Nash and me.

"How was I to know you'd be entertaining?" Sonny grinned. "I'm not interrupting anything, I hope?" he asked with a jut of his chin.

He was chewing a raspberry licorice strap, and thrust the gnawed end at me. "Want some?"

I screwed up my nose and pushed his hand away. "Yuck. You're so gross, and yes, you are interrupting. Please go away."

I returned my attention to Nash, who was looking a little, well, terrified if I was being honest. "You okay?" I asked, touching his shoulder.

"He's not a...a werewolf, is he?" he asked, eyes fixed on Sonny.

"Sharp as a tack, this one," Sonny said, with a lopsided grin.

I shook my head. "No."

"So what is he?"

"I'm a Scorpio," Sonny said, chuckling.

"On the cusp of asshole," I muttered, and inched away from them both. "Tsk, tsk. You have quite the potty mouth, don't you?" Sonny said. "Such a shame."

"No, the real shame is that you're here, ruining a perfectly pleasant evening," I shot back.

Nash still looked a little piqued, but I could tell by the way his breathing steadied and his heartbeat returned to normal that he was relaxing.

And yes. I could hear his heart beat. Weird, I know.

"So, aren't you going to introduce us?" Sonny asked, sizing Nash up. "I don't believe I've had the pleasure."

"No. Just go away."

"Steven Nash," Nash said, extending his hand before I got the chance to stop him. Sonny, being a gigantic douche canoe, just stared at it.

"*Doctor* Steven Nash." I nudged Sonny. "Be polite for once and shake his damn hand," I whispered in his ear.

Sonny conceded, taking Nash's hand and shaking it firmly. A little too firmly if Nash's flinch was anything to go by.

"Ease up, cowboy," I said. "They're surgeon's fingers you're breaking."

"Ahhhh, so this is the transplant doctor you and Vincent were talking about?" Sonny asked, releasing Nash's hand.

I nodded.

"He's looking pretty healthy for someone who was gutted like a fish."

"That's what I thought… Speaking of which, anyone ever tell you your intel sucks? I mean it was way off. You might want to mention it to Vincent."

"I highly doubt that."

"Who's Vincent?" Nash asked, flexing his fingers, which were still clearly smarting after Sonny's exuberant handshake.

"Vincent is the head of—"

Sonny slapped his hand across my mouth. "He's the guy I work for."

"And what kind of work is that?" Nash asked.

"He's one of the Men in Black," I said after I'd pried Sonny's hand from my face. He flashed me a look that could have withered a pitchfork.

"Men in Black?" Sonny asked. "What have you done, Clarissa?"

"Nothing. Well, I did tell Nash about the paranormal stuff, and the POOs, but that's it."

Sonny's emerald eyes blazed with anger. "Please tell me you're kidding," he barked.

I shook my head slowly

"Why would you do that? Can't you just follow the rules?"

"What, like it's *Fight Club* or something? The first rule of POOs is you don't talk about POOs. The second rule of POOs—"

"This isn't a joke, Clarissa."

"Which is why I'm not laughing."

"Vincent is going to pitch a fit when he finds out what you've done."

"That's fine. It wouldn't be the first time and I'm sure it won't be the last."

Nash had gone conspicuously quiet, and one look at his face told me he was both startled and, dare I say it, fanboying a little.

"Are you okay?" I asked, waving my hand in front of his childlike, wide-eyed stare. "Do you need a drink or something?"

"I'm fine. I'm just... I mean, is he really one of the Patron guys?"

I pursed my lips. "Unfortunately, yes."

"Outstanding," Nash said. "I've never met a real-life superhero before."

Sonny looked at me and raised his brows. "Is this guy for real?"

"Of course, he is," I said. "Now, if you don't mind, we were—"

"Never mind what you *were* doing. What I want to know is why you took it upon yourself to share top-secret information with a complete stranger?"

"Firstly, he's not a complete stranger. He's my, um, friend. And secondly, I told him because he's involved and has a right to know."

"Ah, no he doesn't," Sonny said.

"I don't?" Nash asked.

"No—Yes," Sonny and I said simultaneously.

"You're kidding, right?" I said. "Of course he has the right to know. He saw the werewolves, he was attacked and almost killed by one."

"We have ways of taking care of that kind of thing, Clarissa."

"I know, the kadjigoogoos or whatever."

"You can joke with me, woman, but you won't get away with it for that long. When Vincent finds out—"

"*When Vincent finds out. When Vincent finds out,*" I mocked. "You're like a damn parrot. Just don't tell him, and he won't find out. I won't say anything. Nash won't say anything, right?"

"Right," Nash nodded.

"Okay, then. There you have it. Problem solved." I stared at Sonny, willing him to just give the whole thing a rest and stop making a big deal out of a small situation. Did he really have to rush back to him every time I did something stupid and dob on me? "Right?"

Sonny remained silent for a few moments, concentrating so hard, I could almost hear the cogs spinning in his head. Finally, he relaxed. "Fine," he said. "I won't say anything…for now. But you and me, we're going to talk."

"Fine. We'll talk. Whatever. Now that we have that sorted, why don't you just do your magic, poofing thing, and move on to the next person you have to annoy?"

Of course, Sonny didn't do any poofing. Instead, he peered down at my laptop and scrunched up his nose."

"So, what were you two up to anyway?" he asked. "Playing games on the interwebs? Looking up porn?"

I rolled my eyes. "If you must know, I was doing some research."

"Oh yeah? On what?"

"Actually, I was hoping to find out more about my heart donor."

"And how's that going? Got anything interesting?"

"I've only just started."

"So, nothing, then? I knew this whole internet thing wasn't all it was cracked up to be. Just a bunch of D&D geeks with nothing better to do with their time."

He was goading me. I knew it, but I wasn't going to bite. Much.

I tapped a few keys on my laptop and spun it around to face Sonny. He peered at the screen. "Read," I said. "Assuming you can read."

"I can read just fine, thank you," Sonny said.

"Then be my guest." I gestured to the laptop. His lips started moving silently. "Out loud, if you don't mind."

Sonny peered at me, but started reading again, from the beginning. "Patrons of Order, The (see also, Protectors of Terra, Guardians of the Flame, Order of the Peacekeepers) is a powerful and closely guarded organization established in France in the early twelfth century. Reportedly founded by a cooperative consisting of religious, political, paranormal, and industrial pioneers in the first century, the Patrons of Order was established for the purpose of secretly managing the coexistence of humans and paranormal beings across the globe. The head of the organization is purported to be a direct descendent of Aed Mac Cinaeda, a Pictish prince who was killed by known associates in 878AD..."

Sonny stopped reading and looked up at me, eyes wide as saucers. "What is this?"

I pointed to the top of the screen.

"What's a *Wikipedia*?" Sonny asked.

"It's an online platform people use to share information about pretty much any subject—"

"Why?" Sonny growled.

"Well, it's like an encyclopedi—"

"No. I mean why would you do this? Why would you make this information public? Telling Dr. Boy Scout here is one thing, but to make our secrets accessible to pretty much anyone with a computer, that's treason. Not to mention you've put as all in a world of danger."

"You think I put this up?"

"Didn't you?"

"Don't be ridiculous. Of course not." I crossed my arms over my chest.

"If not you, then who?"

"Someone who's not me. I told you, you can find anything on the internet if you know where to look"

"Take it down. Take it down right now," Sonny said, jabbing his finger at the screen, his face going all ruddy. It wasn't his best look.

"I didn't put it up, so I can't take it down."

Sonny swung around, grabbed my shoulders. "Then find out who did and *make them* take it down," he growled.

"You should probably take your hands off her," Nash said, straightening to his full height.

Sonny turned his head toward Nash. "You still here? Don't you have a frog to dissect or something?"

"Sonny! Don't speak to him like that."

"Or what? You gonna kick my ass?" Sonny asked.

"Actually, I was thinking I might do it myself," Nash said.

Sonny released me and focused his full attention on Nash. "And you'd die trying."

"Maybe. Maybe not. I guess we'll see"

"Oh, will you two quit it?" I shoved them apart. "No one's kicking anyone's anything and no one's dying. Both of you just need to sit down and shut up because I have work to do and I can't do it with you two bickering like a pair of school kids."

Sonny sneered at Nash before snatching up my laptop, closing it, and shoving it into its carry bag. "Come on," he said, taking me by the hand. "We're going."

"Going where?" I pulled my hand from his, and also managed to wrangle the laptop bag off his shoulder at the same time. "And don't touch my stuff. You'll break something with your giant man hands."

"We're going to see Vincent. We have to tell him what you found."

"I haven't found anything yet. I barely got started before you poofed in here and covered everything in glitter."

"What are you talking about? I read it myself. That Wonkiepedic thing knows everything."

Nash snorted. "Wonkiepedic. Pfft."

I glared at him and he immediately lowered his eyes.

"Sonny that was nothing but the most basic of searches. I've got a lot of digging to do before we can go to Vincent with anything solid."

I took the laptop out of its bag and put it back on the table.

"Fine. So, what do you want me to do?" Sonny asked.

"Well, shutting up would be a good start," I replied. "Short of that, a cup of coffee would be nice."

Sonny looked at Nash. "You heard the lady. Make her coffee."

"What? Why me?"

"Do I look like someone who knows my way around a kitchen?" Sonny asked.

"No. You look like someone who knows very little about—"

"You know what?" I said, slamming the laptop shut and standing so quickly, my chair toppled over with a loud clatter. "Forget the coffee. Forget the everything. I would like the two of you to leave."

Nash righted the toppled chair and pushed it back under the table.

"I'm not moving from this kitchen," Sonny said. "So, get that idea right out of your head."

"Well, if he's staying, I'm staying," Nash said, pulling the chair out again and plonking himself down.

"Neither of you are staying."

"I think we are," Nash replied.

"What he said," Sonny added, thumbing in Nash's direction.

"Now you're *siding with each other*?" I blew out an exasperated breath. "Fine. You two stay. I'll go."

I scooped everything back up again and trudged toward the door.

"You can't go," Sonny said. "You live here."

"Well, either you leave or I leave," I said. "You choose."

Talk about a standoff.

"Fine. We'll go," Nash said.

"Will we, now?" Sonny asked.

Nash nodded. "I for one know when I've outstayed my welcome."

"You are being a bit of a third wheel, mate."

"Third wheel, my ass," Nash said. "Remember who was invited, and who just flounced in here."

"Ohmygod, neither of you were invited, so both of you get out." I put my stuff back down on the table and shoved them both toward the door. "Out. Out. *Out!* And don't come back until I ask you to. Capisce?"

SIX

THE FIRST TIME I SAW POPPY'S GHOST, I was in the laundry sorting out the colors from the whites, and trying to decide between cooking Pork Dan Dan for dinner, or ordering pizza. I was leaning heavily toward pizza because, who can resist its gooey, oozy deliciousness? Not me, that's who.

I was deep in thought about the Patrons and Vincent and Sonny and Nash and French fries dipped in chocolate milkshake (it's a thing. Chocolate and salt go really well together. Google it.), when I caught a glimpse of something dark and wispy fluttering near the back door.

It was Miss Miranda, who'd come to drop a present for mummy off in her litter tray. How a creature that only weighed four kilos and was all of twenty-centimeters tall, floofy tail notwithstanding, could drop a turd the size of Uluru and stink the house out like last week's green waste, I'd never know. Yet, every day, she made her special deposit and sauntered away like she'd brought me a bunch of daisies. I'm also pretty sure she laughed every time I gagged as I shoveled clumps of dirty kitty litter into an old plastic shopping bag (it's important to reduce, reuse and recycle, kids) that almost always split open mid-poop scoop, scattering cat crap e-v-e-r-y-where.

Scooping the poop was exactly what I was doing when I turned around, turd-filled plastic bag in hand, and saw my sister's ghost floating not three feet away from me.

The last time I'd seen Poppy, we were fourteen and she was, well, dead. Although technically she was still dead, I guess, and she still looked like she was fourteen.

Naturally, the moment I saw her, I screeched like Steve Tyler with his nuts in a vise, and tossed the kitty poop bag in the air, which is exactly how I ended up with cat nuggets and clay pellets aaaaall over the laundry.

If seeing Poppy's ghost floating above my dirty knickers wasn't disturbing enough, add to it the image of Miss Miranda exiting the laundry and passing straight *through* Poppy on her way out. But not without stopping for a quick scratch behind the ears first.

Poppy obliged her, of course—she always did love animals —and Miss Miranda purred and meowed her appreciation. She was such a duplicitous little wench. Miss Miranda, not Poppy. If it wasn't bad enough that my cat obviously didn't love me anymore—not that she loved me any less, come to think of it— now she was sucking up to my dead sister's ghost and mooching pats from her.

Flirt.

Once satiated, Miss Miranda sauntered out of the laundry and in the direction of the lounge room, where she would presumably flop down and sun herself near the glass sliding doors. She was nothing if not a creature of habit.

I, however, was left alone with my sister's ghost and a pile of doona covers that needed depooping.

"I-I-I—" I stammered, backing away as far as I could. "Poppy?" My voice quivered from a combination of mild hysteria and sheer terror, but also a little from annoyance, because now there was cat shit all over my Sheridans.

My sister's solemn-faced ghost nodded.

"What... What do you want?" I asked.

Poppy raised her hands and drifted back and forth. "I want..." Her voice was ethereal and echoed through the small laundry room like a choir singing, *What a Friend We Have in Jesus*, at Sunday mass. "I want your sooouuul," she said.

I blanched. "My *what*?"

"Your *sooouuul*," she repeated, slowly, deliberately. "So that I may finally rest. We are two halves of a whole. I cannot rest until yooouuu rest."

I stared at what could have been my very own reflection, if my reflection were really pale and transparent. Strangely, it was equal parts terrifying and comforting. I'd never felt more confused in my life, and that's saying something because I live most of my life in a constant state of confusion. I was effectively a high-functioning train wreck.

"What do you mean until *I* rest?"

"I need your soul," Poppy warbled. "Give it to me."

"I don't see how that would be possible—"

"Or I'll take it from you."

She was fading in and out like one of those flickery holograms you'd see in an old sci-fi movie, almost disappearing completely before coming back into crisp focus. It was making me feel a bit woozy.

"*Take* it from me?" I gaped. "As in, *kill* me?"

"Yesssss," she hissed. "Kill you."

"Are you serious?" I shrieked. "I mean, I love you. I miss you every single day, but if you think for a split second that I'm going to let you kill me, or worse, kill *myself*, you've got another thing coming—"

Poppy paused for a brief moment before throwing her head back and roaring with laughter which, much to my surprise and relief, was neither terrifying nor menacing. In fact, it was quite melodic and beautiful.

Hm.

Why was Poppy laughing?

Did I say something funny?

I didn't think I had.

Or had I?

"Of course not," she said, between snorts. "Don't be so gullible, Clarissa. I am literally *all* soul. Why in the heck would I want yours?"

You know when you're dreaming and it's one of those really scary ones, and you should be shitting yourself, but you feel okay about it because on some level you know it's only a nightmare, and any minute you know you'll wake up and it'll all be over? Yeah, well, that's kind of how I felt at that moment, only I wasn't dreaming, I couldn't wake up, and I certainly wasn't going to feel better about anything anytime soon because, as I'd discovered over the past few days, dreams *can* actually hurt you.

I brandished the dustpan I was still clutching, courtesy of Miss Miranda's latest deposit, and swung it back and forth in front of myself like the ground crew at the airport waving a jumbo into a hangar.

This only made Poppy laugh harder.

"Oh my God, Lissy. You're hilarious. You haven't changed one bit."

Tears pricked the backs of my eyes at the mention of my childhood nickname. *Lissy.* No one ever called me Lissy except Poppy, and hearing her say it for the first time in a dozen years was, well, let's just say it was just about all I could take.

Poppy stopped laughing when she realized I was crying and rushed to my side. And by rushed, I mean she floated quickly.

"Oh hey, come on. I'm sorry. There's no need for that," she said, reaching out to comfort me. "I was only kidding around."

I brushed her hand away and she dissolved into tendrils of smoke right before my eyes. Only it wasn't exactly smoke. It was— what the hell were ghosts even made of? Fog? Dry ice? Vape? (Although she didn't smell of mixed berries or bubble gum, so I doubt that it was anything to do with vaping.) I certainly didn't know, and I didn't want to, either. What I did want was to get away from the latest nightmare served up by my shiny new paranormal life and crawl into bed...with a tub of Ben and Jerry's...and Netflix.

Desperate for air, I pushed past (or rather, through) Poppy and staggered into the kitchen.

I felt hot, and dizzy, like I was either going to throw up or fall down. Blood was thundering in my ears, pounding through my veins, screaming through every square inch of my body, and I was convinced my heart was about to explode right out of my chest. It was a feeling I'd had a few times of late.

I made it to the sink just in time for my breakfast to come back up, which can I say, was nowhere near as pleasant coming out as it was going in.

With hot tears streaming down my cheeks, and bile burning the back of my throat, I splashed cold water on my face and forced myself to take several deep, calming breaths. My head was throbbing, I had the shakes and I wasn't sure, but I think I might have peed myself a little.

Not my finest moment.

When I was done yacking up my omelet and coffee, I turned and found I was alone in the kitchen, and breathed a sigh of relief.

What the hell had just happened?

Was I asleep?

Was I dreaming?

Was I hallucinating?

Was I drunk?

I glanced at the clock on the microwave: 10:47 a.m. All those options were possible, but it wasn't likely I was drunk this early in the day.

With measured, deliberate steps, I inched my way across the kitchen, and peeked back into the laundry. Other than the pile of sheets covered in cat poop, it was empty.

A wave of relief washed over me, and I sagged to the floor. Maybe I hadn't seen Poppy's ghost, after all? Maybe I'd imagined the whole thing? I'd been under a lot of stress—no one could argue otherwise—and stress can trigger hallucinations, right? Nash had said as much. Plus, I was pretty sure I was getting my period, so I could be forgiven for imagining that the ghost of my dead sister was haunting me, while I was sorting my washing into piles, right?

"I'm not a hallucination," Poppy said, and once again, I shrieked, springing to my feet, and spinning around, wondering just how many times I could do that before I would have a heart attack. I mean, I'd never had any trouble with my donor heart before, but everything had its limits.

"Your heart is fine. You'll never have to worry about that ever again," Poppy said, an unusual look on her face, like she knew a secret I wasn't privy to. I'd seen it many times before, like when she'd watched a new episode of *Veronica Mars* without waiting for me.

I clenched my teeth, closed my eyes and took several deep breaths. "You are not real," I said. "You are not real."

"Oh, come on. That didn't work with Azrael and it's certainly not going to work with me."

I opened my eyes and stared her down. "Does *everyone* know about Azrael?"

"Oh, Lissy, you didn't think you were the only person he visited, did you?"

"Well, actually, yeah. Kind of."

She chuckled and shook her head. "Don't feel bad. He gets around. He's not exactly a one-dying-kid-at-a-time kind of guy."

"Bastard," I grumbled, straightening myself out.

Poppy drifted to the side and let me pass. I headed into the lounge and straight for the liquor cabinet. I needed a stiff drink and I needed it immediately. 10:47 a.m. be damned.

"I love your place," Poppy said, floating around the lounge, stopping to admire the set of authentic Japanese glass fishing floats I ordered through Coastal Vintage. "So much nicer than Mum and Dad's. This is so airy and light, like that beach place we used to go to when we were kids. The one in Sorrento with the porch swing."

I drained my first glass of whiskey, refilled it, and drained it a second time. The liquor burned my throat and made my head light.

Good.

Exactly what I was hoping it would do.

"And you use all the rooms. Not a formal lounge or parlor in sight."

"It's a two-bedroom town house, Pops. There's hardly space for a formal—" I shook my head and refilled my glass again. "No. I'm not doing this. I'm not having a conversation about floor plans with my dead sister."

"You seem really fixated on the fact that I'm dead," she said, crossing her arms. "What's with that?"

"Well, you have to admit this is all a bit weird. I mean, all of a sudden, out of the blue, here you are—"

"But I've always been here," she said, smiling.

"—and we're talking about decor and—wait, *what*? What do you mean you've always been here?"

"I mean, I never left."

"But I've only lived here three years."

"Not here, here, dufus," she said, pointing to the ground. "I mean, here. With you." She pointed at me.

My mouth opened and closed again and I had a sudden, sharp pain in my right temple. I hoped I wasn't having an aneurysm.

That would suck big time. Actually, scratch that. It wouldn't suck at all. It'd fix all my problems and explain a lot. I hoped it was an aneurysm.

"So, when you say, *with me*, you mean, *always* with me? Literally?"

"Sure," she said as she perused my DVD collection. Miss Miranda, the traitorous wench, noticed Poppy floating near the TV cabinet and padded over to her. As Poppy bent down, Miss Miranda flopped on her back and offered up her perfectly floofy belly for rubs. My sister obliged and my cat purred and stretched and made little air biscuits (you know, when they do that kneading thing with their paws—too cute). The last time I tried to rub her belly, Miss Miranda *ffft, ffft, ffft*-ed at me and it took a week for the scratches to heal.

"But you don't actually mean *all* the time, right?"

Poppy stopped scratching a certain belly and looked up at me. "And what if I did actually mean *all the time*? Got a problem with that?"

"No, siree," I said.

Panic.

Rising.

"Well, then there's nothing to worry about then, is there?"

"Who's worried?" I said, wondering if it was a 24/7 always-with-me thing, or if I got private toilet privileges. "I was just asking."

"Of course. I mean, it's not like you've got anything to hide, right?"

"Of course not."

"Not even in your top drawer..."

"Erm..."

"Let's say, behind your bras."

"You've been snooping!" I said, swinging around and pointing an accusatory finger at her. "How many times have I told you to keep your sticky nose out of my stuff?"

"I wasn't snooping."

"Oh, really?" I said, planting my fists on my hips.

"You left your drawer open."

"And what, all my bras just happened to move out of the way and you just happened to see my...my..." I looked away out of sheer humiliation.

"Your autographed photo of Robert Pattinson?"

I whimpered. "Yes."

"That you used to kiss goodnight."

My cheeks turned crimson.

"And cuddle." She waggled her eyebrows and laughed.

"You are such a snoop!" I said in a whiney tone I hadn't used since I was twelve. "You're in so much trouble!"

"What are you going to do about it? Tell Mum?" she mocked.

"I might!"

"And how do you suppose that conversation would go?" she asked, smirking like the big jerk she was. "Hey, Mum, so I was having a conversation with Poppy's ghost the other day and I found out she's been foraging through my knicker drawers again. Could you ground her, please?"

She had a point.

SEVEN

"SO, SOMETHING WEIRD HAPPENED TODAY," I said, watching Azrael wrestle something that looked like an angry octopus from the engine bay of his prized HK Monaro. While I wasn't much of a car chick, I had to admit the black muscle car did look pretty boss with its mirror-finish duco, twenty-one-inch Yokohama rims and chrome-plated twin exhaust.

It looked especially impressive next to my canary-yellow MG hatchback.

Azrael had taken to spending time with me again, a lot of time in fact, just like he had when I was a kid. It wasn't unusual to find him hanging out in my lounge or tinkering on his car. It was nice having him around, it made me feel safe again, knowing he was there protecting me, watching over me. It was comforting.

Of course, this time, I was smart and didn't tell my Mum or Dad he'd come back. The last thing I needed was to spend more time on Dr. Huon's couch while she tried to analyze why I was hallucinating again. Especially since I knew for sure this time I wasn't.

"And what's that?" Azrael said without looking up from the pristine engine bay. Sometimes I thought he liked that car better than he liked me.

"Huh? Oh. Well, I...sort of saw Poppy."

Azrael turned his head in my direction and arched an eyebrow. "Poppy?" he said. "As in—"

"My sister."

"Your *dead* sister?"

"Geez, harsh much? Yes, my *dead* sister."

He stood and wiped his oily hands on the rag he'd tucked into the back pocket of his jeans and folded his arms across his chest. "Where?"

"In the laundry. Scared the pants off me. I may have shrieked a little." I chose not to tell him about the vomiting and the peeing, for my dignity's sake.

"A little?"

"Okay, a lot. Miss Miranda didn't seem to mind—"

"And this happened in broad daylight?"

"Well, yes," I said, trying to ignore how rudely he'd interrupted my retelling of how I'd seen a bonafide, genuine poltergeist. "As I was saying, Miss Miranda—"

"That's, well, extraordinary," he said.

"Miss Miranda?"

"No. The ghost."

"See, that's what I thought. She just appeared out of nowhere, which, as I was saying, didn't seem to bother Miss Miranda at all. I mean, you know how much of a pat-slut she is. But for me, it was like *hooollllyyyyyy shiiiiiit*, you know? It was weird. Plus, I guess I always just thought ghosts were more of a night-time thing."

"They usually are," he said, his expression changing from intrigue to concern in the blink of an eye.

"Anyway," I said, stamping down the niggling feeling something strange was going on; something stranger than the new strange I was growing accustomed to and was rapidly becoming my new normal and not strange at all. "It was so weird. For some reason, I thought she'd look the same as she had when she died, but—"

Azrael was squinting at me, studying me like I was a puzzle begging to be solved.

"What?" I asked.

"How hard did you get hit on the head?" he asked, leaning in close and peering into my eyes.

I leaned back and scowled at him. "What are you talking about?"

"The werewolf attack. How hard did you hit your head?"

"Not that hard. I got bitten, scratched, flung around like a chew toy, but there was no major head injury, just a little bruising, and of course, the claw marks." I turned around, pulled up my t-shirt and presented my back to him for inspection. "But even they're practically gone."

Azrael wasn't even interested in looking at my back. Instead, and much to my surprise, he reached out and buried his hands in my hair, rubbing his fingers across my scalp. I was glad he'd wiped the grease off his hands first, at least.

"Um, what are you doing?" I asked, trying not to feel weirded out.

"Looking for bumps or lacerations. Are you sure you didn't get clocked?"

"Positive," I said, reaching up and removing his hands. "Why are you even asking me that?"

"Because you were clearly hallucinating."

"Was I?" What was it with people telling me I was hallucinating? Seriously.

"Yes. Well, almost certainly," he replied.

"I don't think I was hallucinating," I said, wondering why he was having such a hard time believing me. I'd never lied to him. I'd never even exaggerated or embellished. Okay, well maybe not *never*, but rarely. That he knew about, anyway. So, why wouldn't he believe me now? "Unless hallucinations talk to you and pat your cat."

Azrael gawked at me. "Wait, she actually spoke to you?"

"Yes, she spoke to me, and can I tell you, it was more than a little distressing. The freak-out factor alone..." I shuddered to illustrate my point.

"So, you saw Poppy's ghost, in broad daylight, and she talked to you and made physical contact with your—"

"Cat. Yes. Didn't I just say that?"

Azrael's brow furrowed and his lips thinned. "Well, that's just...unbelievable," he said. "I just don't... *Wow*."

I was taken aback. Azrael really didn't believe me. He actually thought I was lying. I was hurt, and offended, and a little peeved. I didn't deserve that level of mistrust.

"You know," I said. "Given what you do and who you are, I would have thought you of all people might be more inclined to believe in ghosts."

"Of course I believe in ghosts," he replied

I gaped at him. "Oh," I snapped. "So, you just don't believe *me*, then?"

"It's not that I don't believe you, per se," he replied. "It's just, communicating with spirits, actually seeing and being able to talk to them, that's a big deal, Clarissa. Humans just don't have those kinds of abilities."

"What are you talking about?" I said, crossing my arms. I didn't like his tone or what he was implying. "There are heaps of people who communicate with the dead. There were like a gajillion of them at the *Mind Body Spirit* festival last year."

Azrael chuckled. "Yeah, okay."

"What? It's true. I saw this one psychic who told me I was going to meet a man, she called him my prince actually. She said that he'd bring adventure and sunshine into my life. She said he would be full of surprises, work in security and—"

"And?"

"And it totally came true! I mean, not *exactly* like she said— not word for word. The guy's last name was *Duke*, which is kind of like prince, and he was *from* Sunshine. And okay, so he wasn't so much in security as he was a small-time drug dealer *dodging* security, but I didn't know that when he slid into my DMs. And he really did change my life. I'm not on *eLovestory* or any other matchmaking sites anymore because, you know, drug dealer. And okay, so she may have gotten his physical description completely wrong, and now that I'm saying all this with the benefit of hindsight, I'm beginning to think maybe she was a fake after all."

That puzzled look Azrael sometimes got when I was talking crept over his face and I figured it was as good a time as any to shut up.

"As I was saying, they interpret body language and do cold readings, Clarissa," he said. "And they're damn good at it. They take advantage of vulnerable, desperate people all the time, so don't feel bad for getting sucked in."

"Well, I wasn't feeling bad before," I muttered, trying to remember how many people I'd told the psychic story.

Dr. Jade.

Miss Lisa.

Drew.

Mum.

Rhonda from my Pilates group.

That chick with the blue hair from the deli.

Urgh. Too many.

"Truth be told, I can't remember the last time I came across a human who was a genuine medium," Azrael said.

"Really?" Maybe I really had been hallucinating?

"Truly." He nodded. "This kind of thing in a human is as rare as rocking horse shit. And usually they only have it because they've got some latent paranormal gene."

"Latent?"

"Recessive. Dormant. However you prefer to put it."

If what he was saying was true, it meant that thanks to my werewolf heart, I wasn't totally human anymore. That certainly didn't please and sparkle.

"So, do you have any idea how I got it? The clairvoyance, I mean. Could it be a side effect, you know, from the werewolf heart?"

"Maybe, but it's not really a werewolf trait. Vampires, faeries, seers obviously, but it's not really a lycan thing."

"Okay, well, how long will it last?"

"It isn't viral. You don't just catch it, and you certainly don't just get rid of it."

"So, what are you saying? This is *permanent*?"

Azrael shrugged. "Beats me."

I grabbed him by the collar and dragged him down, so we were face-to-face. "You don't understand. This was not a pleasant experience for me," I said. "I'm not sure my nerves could handle this much longer. You have to help me!"

"Well, I guess the Patrons might know," he squeaked, trying to extricate himself from my vise-like grip. "You could ask them."

I let go of his collar, dropped my shoulders, threw back my head and mock-cried. "But I don't want to talk to them," I whined. "They're awful, awful people."

"Can't argue with that," he said, straightening himself. "But I also think they'll know more about this than anyone."

"This is so unfair! Why do I have to talk to them? It's not like any of this is my fault."

"Of course it's not your fault."

"Then why are you punishing me?"

"Stop being a baby. No one's punishing you. Like I said, the only ones who can help get to the bottom of this are the Patrons. You have to reach out to them."

I huffed. "Yeah, well, if I have to talk to them, then you're coming with me."

Azrael laughed. It was a hearty laugh that reverberated through his whole body. It was a sound I normally enjoyed. But not today.

I cocked my brow and he sobered.

"Oh, you're serious."

"Of course I'm serious," I said.

"Okay, then," he replied with a shrug. "Why not?"

"Good. We'll go see the stupid Patrons, and we'll listen to all their stupid theories. But it won't do any good," I said. "No good, I'm telling you."

"Well, then, I guess we'll find out, won't we?" He turned his attention back to his angry octopus.

Stupid Azrael with his stupid logic and stupid car. I turned around and marched toward the house, slammed the front door and skulked up the stairs, before throwing myself, 50s movie-Siren style, onto my bed and sobbing into my pillow.

EIGHT

"SO, WHAT'S HIS STORY ANYWAY?"

"Who?" Azrael asked, grabbing the bag of fast food I'd ordered from the drive through, and passing it across the console to me.

"Vincent," I said with a smile. "He said he's human, but he's also like, a gajillion years old. Practically prehistoric. So, I'm guessing he's what, a vampire?"

Azrael screwed his face up in what I could only presume was disgust. "Oh, good God, no," he said with a shudder. "Nothing like that. Vampires are vile, loathsome creatures. All they care about is sex, blood, and seduction. Vincent, on the other hand, is above them. Actually, he's pretty much above everyone."

Okay, so, firstly, turns out vampires, really not so popular with the Inner World folk, although I had to admit I didn't mind the sound of all that carnal sex and seduction stuff. I made a mental note to ask Azrael about that some other time.

Secondly, Azrael seemed to be fanboying all over Vincent, just like Sonny had. What was with that guy? Was he the Dave

Grohl of the Inner World? If he was, for the life of me I couldn't understand why. Maybe if I got to know him better?

"So, what then?" I asked.

"Curse," Azrael replied, taking a sip from a takeaway cup of soft drink. "A big, fat, you're-screwed-til-the-end-of-time curse."

I nodded and stuffed a handful of French fries into my mouth. I was starving, all the time, thanks to yet another shiny new, post-death side effect I'd developed.

"Whof kind off curff waff it?" I asked, chewing my fries feverishly.

"God, woman. Weren't you taught that it's rude to speak with a full mouth?"

I swallowed and cleared my throat. "Sorry," I said. "What kind of curse was it?"

"No one really knows for sure. The story goes Vincent is a Pictish prince, betrothed even before birth to marry a princess from another clan."

"Peckish? What does that even mean? Was he hungry all the time? Because I totally understand that."

"Pictish." Azrael laughed. "Pict-ish."

It sounded like he expected me to know what Pictish meant. Maybe I should. Maybe, if I'd paid closer attention in Mr. Camm's Weird Shit from Around the World class (otherwise known as History 101), I wouldn't be asking these stupid questions.

Urgh.

"Earth to Clarissa." Azrael waved a hand in front of my face. "Helloooo."

"Yes, Pictish. Gotcha. That's…um, so cool. I've always wanted to go to, err… Pict…land…dia?"

"You know nothing about the Picts, do you?" Azrael asked, easing the Monaro onto the freeway, and gunning the engine. The G-force pushed me back in my seat as the 308 rumbled to life. Who doesn't love the sound of a fully worked V8 when it got out on the open road? It was like a giant cat purring.

I hung my head. "Nope. Can't say that I do."

He chuckled. "The Picts came from Scotland."

"Is that so? How far back are we talking?" I asked.

"Um, 600 AD-ish."

Wowsers. Vincent really *did* look good for his age. I wondered who his dermatologist was. "So, what happened? I mean, I presume he didn't marry the princess?"

"Uh, no. Vincent did a bad, bad thing. He fell in love with another woman. A peasant girl. Someone not of his caste."

"This isn't going to end well, is it?"

Azrael shook his head. "He refused to marry the princess, and let's say that didn't go over too well with her family."

"So, they cursed Vincent?"

"No. They murdered the peasant girl."

"Geez," I said, frowning. "Harsh."

"That's not the half of it. The girl's clan, they were completely distraught and wanted cold-blooded revenge. Not only did they murder every single member of the princess's clan, they also killed everyone in Vincent's clan, and then cursed Vincent himself."

"I don't like this story," I said with a pout.

"The way they saw it, it was Vincent's fault their daughter was dead. So, they evoked the maledictions for smiting evildoers and, well, curse."

"Maledictions. Smiting. It's all so…gruesome," I said with a shudder "So what malediction are we talking about?"

"Immortality."

I gasped. "As in, Vincent *can't* die?"

Azrael nodded.

"As in, forever and ever, a life without end?"

"That's what they say."

"Geez, who were these people? They were witches, weren't

they?"

"No idea." Azrael shrugged. "But they cursed him good, and he's been around ever since."

"Wow. That's just..." I frowned. "So, so sad. I mean, here he is, one of the most powerful men in the world, revered by everyone. He's been everywhere, done everything, knows everybody. Nothing's new. Nothing's exciting. And nothing will be again."

"Well, when you put it like that."

"I mean, it's not like he can have any kind of healthy relationship, either. He can't get married or have a family or even lasting friendships, because literally everything and everyone he loves will wither and die right before his eyes. It hurts my heart just thinking about it."

Azrael tilted his head and smiled at me. "You're pretty astute when you want to be, kiddo. You know that, right?"

I shrugged. "I just call 'em as I see 'em."

"You're a good egg," he said, reaching over and ruffling my hair.

"Stop it. You'll give me a big head." I smoothed my hair down. "And screw up my blowout."

Traffic ahead started to get heavy, so Azrael geared down and slowed to a coasting speed. When had traffic gotten so bad in Melbourne? Once upon a time, I'd been able to get from my place to the city in less than thirty minutes. These days I needed a Sherpa and a packed lunch just to get to IKEA.

"One thing I don't understand," I said, opening the top of my hot fudge sundae. "If Vincent is human, why does he seem to have, I don't know, superpowers? I mean, for someone who is human, he's not particularly human at all."

"I guess after 1,500 years, you develop certain skills. Plus, he's a seer—"

"Seer?"

Azrael frowned at me, a clear sign I was annoying him, "He's learned to read and control minds. He performs earth magicks. He can heal himself and others. Can you imagine?" Azrael asked.

"I think it's safe to say I can't." I licked chocolate sauce off my little plastic spoon and sighed with delight. "And what about Sonny?"

"What about him?"

"What's his backstory?"

"No idea. All I know is that he's a Peacekeeper and has been for a few centuries. He's a skilled warrior, and he's utterly devoted to serving Vincent and the Patrons."

Azrael geared down again, and slowly edged his way along with the afternoon traffic.

"He's also a notorious lothario and, to the best of my knowledge, Vincent is the only person who knows Sonny's backstory. Although, if you ask me, it sounds like a bunch of hooey. He's probably just a vampire."

"Hooey?" I laughed. "Is it 1962 all of a sudden?"

I tried to ignore the jolt of jealousy that exploded in my heart and skittered into the pit of my stomach when Azrael mentioned Sonny's reputation with the ladies. I really needed to see my doctor about that. Maybe I had developed a murmur? Or reflux, which wasn't beyond the scope of possibility given how much I was eating of late.

Or maybe I was just feeling overwhelmed. This was a lot to take in. A lot to process, a lot to believe. It was just a lot.

We spent the rest of the drive in silence, Azrael concentrating on the traffic, and me staring out the window just trying to process everything.

I wasn't having much luck.

"We're here," Azrael said, pulling up outside St. Francis's.

I looked up at the church and sighed. "It's not too late to change our minds, you know."

Azrael shook his head. "You're not getting out of this one. Come on, let's go see what Vincent has to say about all this."

NINE

GENERALLY SPEAKING, when you render the head of a super-secret organization dedicated to keeping the human race safe from dark forces, speechless, it's not a good sign.

Of course, that's exactly what happened when I told Vincent that I was now, as Azrael put it, communing with the dead.

I had no idea it was such a big deal, but given I'd never known either Vincent or Sonny to be quiet for more than five seconds before, there must have been some truth to it. Although, they could just as easily have been stunned by Azrael's presence and not by the news of my shiny new psychicness, because they had both been super-cagey from the moment we'd walked in, even before I told them about Poppy.

Vincent had been gracious when we arrived, adjourning the meeting he was hosting with the heads of… of…I want to say ChoopaBurras? KookaCabras? Something like that. He offered us refreshments and a seat while he bid farewell to his guests who, PS: smelled a lot like my Aunty Mary's farm. You know, like poop. From the animals, not from Aunty Mary. She had sheep and chickens mostly, but there were also a few goats and a pig named Rosco.

Sonny, on the other hand, had just been rude, barely speaking a word and throwing old-school greasies at Azrael like it was *WrestleMania 3;* he was Hulk Hogan, and Azrael was Rowdy Roddy Piper.

I had no idea why Sonny was being so antagonistic toward Azrael, someone he'd never even met. Not that Azrael seemed to care. All I knew was if I didn't break the tension pronto, I'd probably suffocate from testosterone poisoning.

After Vincent bid his final farewell to the fertilizer-smelling, horned ones, and when I explained the reason for our unannounced visit, he seemed flummoxed.

I seemed to be having that effect on a lot of people lately.

"If you'll excuse us for a few minutes," Vincent said with a grimace. "Sonny and I need to—"

"No," Sonny said, scowling at Azrael. "I'll stay here."

Vincent frowned. "Are you sure? I could really use your help."

"Nope. I'm good."

Vincent sighed. "Alrighty, then." He turned back to me and Azrael, and shrugged. "If you'll excuse me, I need to make a few calls. Privately, you understand. Please make yourselves comfortable and I'll be back as soon as practicable. Sonny will ensure you have everything you need in my absence, right, Sonny?"

Sonny nodded and folded his arms over his chest at the same moment Azrael laced his fingers behind his head, leaned back in his chair, and crossed his legs at the ankles.

They were like a pair of posturing peacocks and personally, I found the whole display a little pathetic.

As he took his leave, Vincent leaned into Sonny and whispered, "Behave."

I briefly wondered why he would say that, and contemplated

asking what he'd meant, but I decided against it. Instead, I fished my phone out of my bag and tapped the Google app. I had homework to do if I was going to convince Azrael or Vincent that not only were psychic humans real, but they were everywhere.

"You know, I sure could use a cold brew right about now. How about you, Riss?" Azrael cooed.

"Riss?" Sonny said, sitting forward. "*Riss?*"

I looked up from my phone. I hadn't really been paying attention to what either of them had been saying. "Huh?"

"He calls you *Riss?*" Sonny asked, with a little more agitation than the situation warranted. "You're on a pet name basis?"

I shrugged. "Sure. I guess so. He calls me a lot of things."

"It's true. I've been known to call her Wheezy Monkey. Doodlebug. Munchkin."

"I haven't been a munchkin in over a decade, Azrael," I said.

"Sometimes, I even call her She-Devil, if she's been particularly naughty," he said with a wink.

"Don't be a dick." I put my phone back in my bag. I realized I had no way of knowing if the psychics' websites were legit, or simply a well-disguised fraud. "One time you called me that. *One* time."

Azrael nodded and chuckled.

I was acutely aware of the uncomfortable tension simmering in the room. It was a feeling that made the hairs on the back of my neck bristle. I didn't understand it, and I definitely didn't like it.

"So," Azrael said, turning his mischievous grin on Sonny. "What about that brewski?"

"What are you talking about?" Sonny sneered.

"You heard the boss. Your job is to make sure we have everything we need, and what I need is a cold one."

"I didn't know you drank?" I said, blinking at Azrael. "Are you even allowed?"

Sonny snorted.

"Allowed? Why wouldn't I be allowed?" Azrael asked.

I shrugged. "I don't know. I guess I wasn't sure that they'd let you."

"*They*? Who are you even talking about?"

"You know," I said, pointing up. "The boss?"

"Nobody tells me what I can and can't do," Azrael snapped.

"I could tell you where to go," Sonny muttered. "Would that help?"

Azrael tossed Sonny a little side-eye shade and sized him up. "What's your problem, man?"

Uh oh.

"Who says I have a problem?"

"Well, I suppose you could actually be a giant jerk to everyone, but somehow I think it might just be reserved for me."

"No, he's actually a jerk," I said, trying to make light of the situation. Neither of them laughed, or even appeared to acknowledge that I was there.

Double uh oh.

Sonny straightened and Azrael slowly rose to his feet. Much to my horror, they were actually squaring up to each other.

Uh oh. Uh oh. Uh oh.

"Who are you calling a jerk?" Sonny asked.

"Well, I don't see any other jerks here."

"I could get you a mirror, if you like?"

"What is your drama? You don't even know me," Azrael sniped.

"I know your kind. You bring nothing but misery and heartache to everyone you touch."

"Oh, because you're the harbinger of joy, are you?"

"Compared to you? Yeah. I'm a jolly surprise."

"You know what?" I said, squeezing myself between their giant frames, and grinning up at them both. "It looks like we may have gotten off on the wrong foot. So, why don't we try this again? How does that sound?"

Neither Sonny nor Azrael said a word, instead just glared at each other.

"Alrighty then, why don't I start with proper introductions? Azrael, this is Sonny," I said. "He's a Peacekeeper, ironically. Sonny, this is Azrael. He's—"

Sonny rolled his eyes and held up his hand with a dramatic flourish. "No introductions needed," he snarked. "I know exactly who he is. All I want to know is why he's here, and feel free to be specific."

"What do you mean, why am I here?" Azrael asked. "Since when do I need a reason to do anything? Unlike you, Peacekeeper, I do what I please."

It was obvious Sonny didn't like Azrael all that much, judging by the low rumble of his voice when he spoke to him. Azrael didn't appear to be enamored with Sonny either, not that I blamed him. Sonny was an obnoxious turd, after all. A perfectly chiseled, superbly sexy, smells like rain and ripe peaches, obnoxious turd that I wanted to climb like a tree. But a turd nonetheless.

Sonny ignored Azrael completely and turned his attention back to me. "So, what's the story?" he asked. "Why did you even bring him here?"

The following forty-seven seconds of my life went something like this:

ME

"Because we thought you or Vincent might have some insight into why I'm suddenly talking to my dead sister."

AZRAEL

"I think the question should be why are *you* here? What function do you even perform?"

SONNY

"I'm trying to protect Clarissa against the likes of you."

ME

"I don't exactly need protecting, thank you. I mean, Azrael has been in my life since I was a kid—"

AZRAEL

"And, aren't you doing a wonderful job of it? She's only died what, twice this week?" [Clapping his hands] "Bravo. Well done, old mate."

SONNY

"If I can stop the likes of you digging your claws into her, I consider it a job well done."

ME

"There really isn't a need for all this aggression, you know. I think maybe we should—"

AZRAEL

"Oh please. You had nothing to do with keeping her safe, and you know it."

SONNY

"Does she even know who you *really* are?"

ME

"Of course, I do. I'm not an idiot."

AZRAEL

"She knows what she needs to know."

SONNY

"Typical. Are you even planning on telling her? Or are you happy to let her find out the old-fashioned way?"

ME

"Are either of you listening to me? I told you I know who Azrael is."

AZRAEL

"That's between me and Clarissa."

ME

"He's my—"

SONNY

"I knew it. You're such a coward. Such a—"

ME
"—Guardian Angel."

The moment the words left my mouth, both Sonny and Azrael fell deathly silent, and gaped at me.

"What?" I said, planting my hands on my hips. "What did I say?"

"What did you call me?" Azrael spluttered, his usually tanned skin paling to the point of translucence.

"My Guardian Angel." I beamed.

Another moment of silence passed before Sonny snorted so loud, I thought he was choking.

Then he started laughing.

And laughing.

It was a hearty, strangely lyrical sound that made his whole body shake, and in turn reverberated through mine in the most delicious way.

"Guardian," Sonny squeaked as he clapped a hand on Azrael's back. "Angel."

"Shut up, Sonny," Azrael barked, shrugging Sonny's hand away. "And get your meat hooks off me."

"Oh, this is just—*priceless*."

"I. Said. Shut. Up," Azrael repeated, punctuating each word with a finger jab to Sonny's chest. They'd somehow squeezed me out from between them and were now toe to toe, chest to chest.

Uh oh x infinity.

"I don't see what's so funny," I said, getting a little annoyed with both of them.

Azrael turned and grasped my shoulders. "Why on earth would you think I was a Guardian Angel?"

I frowned at him and tried to block the sound of Sonny guffawing in my ear.

"Because that's what you are. Or is that not the correct term?

Is Angel not PC? Should I have called you a spirit? Heavenly messenger? I'm not up to speed with the lingo yet—"

"I. Can't. Breathe," Sonny said, bracing himself against the side of Vincent's desk.

Now, he was really pissing me off.

"I mean, you watched over me so many times. You sat with me and kept me safe when I was... When I was..." I looked away, the mere thought of the years of suffering I endured enough to flood my eyes with hot tears.

"*Dying*," he snapped, which was harsher than I expected.

"Yes."

"I can't wait to tell Vincent about this," Sonny wheezed, stretching his arm out and balancing himself on the back of a chair. "He's going to—"

"Do you mind, Sonny?" I asked.

"Not at all," he replied.

"Clarissa, you've got this all wrong," Azrael said, tightly. "I'm not an angel, guardian or otherwise."

I blew out an exasperated breath. "Of course you are. You've got the wings. You do the magic. You have the shimmery eye thing going on. What else could you possibly be?"

"Where's your harp, Angel Boy?" Sonny snarfled.

"I promise you, Sonny," I said. "I'm going to punch you right in the—"

"I'm not your Guardian Angel, Clarissa," Azrael said, as I shook my fist at Sonny.

"Then why would you take such good care of me? Watch over me and keep me safe?"

"I wasn't keeping you safe," Azrael said in a low tone that sounded like he was angry. Why would he be angry? What had I done wrong? "I was there to take you."

I couldn't think of anything I'd done to upset him or—wait, *what*?

I blinked up at him and stepped back. "Take me? *TAKE ME?*

Like in some weird sexual way? Because, wow, yuck. There never was, nor will there ever be, any taking—"

"Whoa! Stop." Azrael held his hands up and cringed. "Just stop. I wasn't talking about taking you that way. Jesus, no. You're not listening to what I'm saying, Clarissa. I'm not an angel," Azrael sobered. "I'm a Reaper. I'm..." He blew out a steadying breath. "I'm Death."

I paused for a second. It sounded like he said Death. That couldn't be right. I must have misunderstood.

"You're deaf?" I asked.

This only made Sonny laugh harder. "Oh, God, please stop. I can't breathe."

"No," Azrael replied. "Not deaf. *Death.*"

"Death. The *Death?*"

"Yes!" he said. "I was never there to protect you. I was just waiting for you to die."

Well, cover me in coconut and call me a lamington. What the hell had I just heard?

"You were waiting for me to die? I don't... I can't... *WHAT?*"

"I told you you should have told her what you were sooner," Sonny said to Azrael.

"You knew about this?" I screeched at Sonny.

"Well, no. I mean, I know what Azrael is. I just didn't know you didn't. I *assumed* he'd told you."

"I assumed she knew!" Azrael yelled. "I mean, how was I to know she didn't understand? All the others—"

"Aha! So Poppy was right. There were others!" I was rapidly verging toward hysteria.

"Um, yes?" Azrael replied.

"You told her she was the only one?" Sonny asked.

"What? No. I didn't tell her anything."

"That's just it. You told me *nothing*! You just let me believe that you were one of the good guys."

"The lady has a point," Sonny said.

"Shut up!" I said. Or screeched. Whatever.

"Yeah, shut up, Sonny."

"You shut up, too." I turned on Azrael. "Both of you just shut your damn mouths. I can't even look at either of you right now, much less listen to the lies spilling from you."

Azrael stepped toward me and reached out. I slapped his hands away. "Don't you dare touch me."

Azrael sagged. "I'm sorry, Clarissa. I thought you knew. I thought—"

"Yeah, well, you thought wrong."

"Why else did you think I came back?"

"That's an excellent question. Why did you come back?" I asked. "Care to explain?"

"Because you died. You know, at the hockey game. You died and I came to get you. I came to take you to the other side."

"But I didn't die, did I?"

"Well, technically, you did. You just didn't stay dead, which is why old mate over here keeps hanging around," Sonny said.

"I really hate you."

"Who?" Azrael asked.

"Both of you. In fact, I hate you both so much, I can't be held responsible for what I'll do to you if I stay here much longer." I gathered my belongings, my coat, my laptop, my handbag and stormed toward the office door. "And if either of you even think of following me, I'll gut you like a fish."

TEN

psychopomp
/ˈsʌɪkə(ʊ)pɒmp/
noun

1 (in Greek mythology) a guide of souls to the place of the dead;
the spiritual guide of a living person's soul.

AFTER I RECOVERED FROM THE SHOCK of learning
Azrael wasn't, in fact, my Guardian Angel, but instead the Grim-
fucking-Reaper who's only reason for spending time with me was
because he was waiting for me to die so he could accompany me to
the Afterworld, I stalked out of Vincent's office to get some fresh air.
Only we were nine stories underground and there was no fresh air to
be had. So, I sat on the floor in the hall outside instead and sobbed.

I could still hear Azrael and Sonny bickering in Vincent's
office; raised voices and things flying around.

"Now, look at what you've done," I heard Sonny say.

"What I've done? You were the one—"

"Why would you just blurt it out like that? She clearly wasn't ready to hear it."

"I thought she knew!"

"How would she know? Unless you told her?"

Listening to them ping-pong back and forth was both exhausting and humiliating.

How much of a chump was I, believing in Guardian Angels and that Azrael was my friend? He wasn't my friend. He was a fraud, and the only reason he'd come back into my life now wasn't to keep me safe, but because I was dying all the damn time. I was just a job to him.

I heard footsteps approaching from the right, and lifted my head, wiping the tears from my eyes. Blurry Vincent was standing next to me.

"Everything okay?" he asked with a frown.

I didn't reply, only kept sniffling and gurgling like a drain.

"Obviously not," he said, crouching down and joining me on the cold parquetry floor.

"Your trousers will get dirty," I snuffled, pointing at the Paul Smith pants he wore.

Vincent shrugged. "I don't mind. They're only pants."

Seven-hundred-dollar designer pants.

"So, would you like to tell me what happened in there? I could hear the yelling all the way up on five."

I sighed and gurgled. "Azrael is the Grim Reaper."

"Yes, well, I guess you could call him that," Vincent said. "And this is new information for you?"

I nodded.

"Can I ask what you thought he was?"

No sooner had I uttered the words Guardian Angel, Vincent snorted, not quite as loud as Sonny had, but it was a snort, nonetheless. After I glared at him, he at least had the decency to cover the laugh with a fake cough.

"And this has upset you?" Vincent said, regaining his self-control.

"Of course it has upset me. I thought Azrael was my friend. I thought he was looking after me. Do you have any idea how embarrassing this is?" I whined.

"Why would it be embarrassing?" Vincent asked.

"Because I'm obviously an idiot. I should have known who he was. *What* he was. I should have realized—"

"What on earth makes you think either of those things should have occurred to you? You were a child. You were scared and alone and Azrael offered you comfort."

"Little did I know that he had an ulterior motive," I replied.

"I don't think he did, to be honest," Vincent said in that beautifully soothing tone he used. "He was under no obligation to show you kindness or love. He's a psychopomp. His only obligation is to offer you safe passage to the place of the dead. Yet, he chose to watch over you, to be your friend. I think that's telling."

"Yeah, it tells me I'm clearly some sort of charity case, a gullible fool."

Vincent rolled his eyes. "Now you're just looking for pity."

"Do you blame me?"

"What I was trying to say, Mademoiselle Overactive Imagination, is I think it's telling about *Azrael*, not you. He obviously cared—correction, *cares*—about you. He wanted you to know you were loved, and not to be afraid."

"He wanted to kill me."

"No," Vincent said firmly. "That's not what he does. He doesn't cause death. He's not a killer. He's a guide."

"He's a liar."

"Did he actually tell you he was your Guardian Angel?"

I thought back real hard. Ten years wasn't exactly yesterday, and let's face it, I forget most things at the best of times. So really, asking me to remember conversations from a decade earlier was a stretch. And yet somehow, I think I'd have remembered if Azrael had expressly told he was a Guardian Angel. It's not the kind of thing you simply forget. I guess I'd always just assumed. Just as Azrael had. I sighed.

"No. He didn't," I conceded, because you know what they say about people who assume. It turns you into a donkey or something.

"Then he's not a liar."

"He didn't exactly tell me the whole truth, though, did he?"

"Withholding the truth isn't the same as lying."

"It feels the same," I sighed. "It still hurts."

Vincent reached out and took my hand. "I'm not saying Azrael did the right thing not being honest with you. But what I do know is that he's in there." Vincent pointed to his office door. "And if the yelling is anything to go by, he's feeling pretty remorseful about this entire situation. He probably wishes he could turn back time and take away the pain he's caused."

"Can he actually do that?"

"No. Only one being can do that," Vincent said, pointing upward.

"Please tell me you mean God and not Rebecca?" I groaned.

He smiled and nodded.

I paused and listened as Sonny and Azrael continued to bicker.

"In my experience, Reapers don't usually show any regret."

"Regret?"

"Remorse. Concern. Whatever you want to call it. Azrael is obviously very upset he hurt you. Does it really matter what his job description says? The fact is, he made you feel safe and loved at a time when you really needed it. He might not be your Guardian Angel, but it sounds to me like he was your friend."

I looked at Vincent. He smiled again and squeezed my hand.

Eventually, I conceded. "You know I despise your Earth logic, right?"

"I'm beginning to sense that," Vincent said, reaching into his pocket, pulling out a silk handkerchief, monogrammed of course, and handing it to me. I used it to swipe at my leaky eyes and runny nose and offered it back to him.

"Why don't you keep it?" he said. "I have many."

I clutched the damn square of silk like it was a security blanket and smiled at Vincent. He was totally the guy who wore designer slacks, drank from cut crust glasses and had drawers stuffed full of monogrammed hankies. He was also the guy who sat on the floor and comforted you when you are crying.

"Shall we go back in now, and sort the two of them out?" Vincent asked, standing and offering me his hand. I took it and wobbled to my feet. "Before they start trading blows. I recently remodeled my office and I have a feeling if those two get into it, I'll need to get Ms. Blayze back here to fix things up."

"Miss Blayze, as in, *Shaynna* Blayze?" I asked.

"The one and only."

"You know, I'd go in there and tear your office up myself if it meant meeting Shaynna."

Vincent raised his brows. "If you go in there and sort this situation out, I promise to introduce you to Ms. Blayze myself. No remodeling required."

I thought about it briefly and my heart fluttered with excitement. "Fine," I said, brushing some dust off my butt. "But can we at least pretend I'm still super angry at the two of them? I'd like to see them grovel for a bit longer."

Vincent nodded. "As you wish."

"Thank you," I replied.

I was beginning to really like him.

ELEVEN

"HAVE YOU EVER TRIED GOOGLING YOURSELF?" I asked Vincent after a two-hour conversation where I tried to explain:

1. what I did for a living, and
2. how the digital world worked.

Turns out, explaining Insta Reels and TikTok to a two-thousand-year-old Pictish prince, not so easy.

Sonny and Azrael were long gone after Vincent gave them both a good dressing down. He played the part of the angry, protective father figure quite well. So well, in fact, even I almost believed he was genuinely angry with the two buffoons for blurting out such a sensitive truth and upsetting me so much. Vincent finished his thirty-minute tirade by ordering them out and telling them not to return until they were prepared to beg for my forgiveness, which he believed I was fully entitled not to accept.

That's when I made the rookie mistake of offering to school Vincent on the perks and pitfalls of the digital world.

"I beg your pardon?" Vincent said, eyes widening.

"You know," I replied. "Googling yourself...for fun."

"I have never, nor will I ever, do such a thing. This is a respectable organization, Clarissa. I'm royalty, for heaven's sake. We are not some filthy house of disrepute!"

I eyed him closely. "What exactly do you think Google means?"

"Well, I imagine it's...um. I mean it's probably..." He sighed. "Fine, I have no idea what it means," he replied. "But it sounds lewd and inappropriate."

"I think *you* might be lewd and inappropriate," I said with a smile.

"I am no such thing."

"I beg to differ. You're the one who took a perfectly innocent word and turned it into some kind of weird, sexy-time—"

"Stop," he said, shaking his head. "I concede. What's a Google?"

I chuckled. "It'll be easier if I just show you. Hand over your laptop." I stuck out my hand, prepared to take possession of the device.

"Laptop?" he asked, with the kind of perplexed expression you might expect to see on a puppy looking at itself in the mirror for the first time.

"Yes, laptop. Your portable computer."

"I don't have one."

"Okay, well, can't say I'm completely surprised, but whatever. Point me at your desktop then."

"I don't have one of those, either."

My brows shot up. "Seriously? No desktop? Not even an old Commodore 64 laying around?"

"Yes, seriously. We have no need for computers here. We do things simply—the tried-and-true way."

"I think you mispronounced slow and obsolete," I replied with a grin.

Vincent sighed heavily. "We have done things a particular way for centuries, Clarissa. And even though you seem to think we are little more than cavemen—"

"Possibly because you live in a great big cave?"

"I can assure you we have always experienced great success in all our endeavors—"

"Yes, I've seen firsthand just how successful you've been in endeavoring to sort out my sideshow of a situation."

[Insert massive eye roll]

"And," he continued, completely ignoring my interruptions. "I see absolutely no reason to change things now, purely because you think we're—"

"Archaic? Antiquated? Outmoded?"

"I was going to say old-fashioned."

"And then some," I said. "Look, just give me something to work with. How about a tablet? Surely someone has one laying around?"

"Actually, I might be able to help you with that," he said, rising to his feet. "I can get you a tablet. Actually, I can get you two, but I don't know how useful they'll be."

"Because they're so old they're pretty much prehistoric?"

"Well, yes."

"That's okay. Maybe I can find a workaround to upgrade the operating system, and keep our fingers crossed that we can connect to the Wi-Fi. You do have Wi-Fi down here, don't you?"

"I'm not even going to pretend I understood any of that," Vincent said. "But I trust you know what you're talking about. Can I just ask how the tablets will help you with your gaggle?"

"It's Google."

"Fine. *Goooogle*. Does it have something to do with the markings?"

"Unless you're actually looking for geese, in which case gaggling sounds about right—wait, what markings?"

"The markings on the tablets."

"What on earth did you do to the tablets?"

"I didn't *do* anything. The markings were there when we procured them."

"Ohmygod," I groaned. "You didn't get them off *Buy Swap and Sell* did you? You know half the stuff on there is either fake or stolen...or damaged."

"I have no idea what a Buy Swap and Sell is, but you can rest assured the Vatican procured the tablets from a legitimate source."

"Marketplace is only marginally better, and don't get me started on..."

Um, wait, did he say Vatican? Did Mark-fricken-Zuckerberg literally own everything these days? Would I be downloading the iPope app so I could go to Easter Sunday mass next year?

I shook my head. Something was amiss. "Okay, I'm confused. Exactly what type of tablets are we talking about here? Apple? Samsung? Acer?"

"Sacred." Vincent looked at me like I was insane, and for a second, I was inclined to believe him.

"Sacred."

"Yes, sacred. Divine. Hallowed."

"I know what sacred means, *Roget*." I pursed my lips and tried to make sense of the conversation with very little success, until I had a teeny-weeny epiphany and the strange truth dawned on me.

"Vincent, the markings on the tablets, what are they?" I asked, still wondering how I even got into this whole weird situation in the first place. I was still hoping I'd wake up and find it was all a bad dream, even though I knew the chances were slim.

"The Ten Commandments," he said so casually, I almost thought he was joking. In fact, I even started laughing.

Of course, he wasn't joking, so I eased up on the chuckles, and literally had to prop myself up on his desk to stop myself from sliding to the floor.

I held my hand up. "I'm sorry, but are you talking about *the* Ten Commandments, like from the *Bible*?"

"Are there any other kind?" he replied.

Fair point.

"As in Noah and the Burning Bush?"

"Moses," Vincent corrected.

"*Whatever.* You're telling me you're in possession of the *actual* stone tablets?"

"Why are you having so much trouble comprehending this?"

I couldn't even begin to know how to answer that, so I ignored the question altogether. "And they're here? In *Melbourne*?" I asked.

"Don't be silly. Of course not."

"Of course not." I shook my head. "What was I thinking?"

"They're in Rome."

"Rome."

"Actually, Vatican City."

"Naturally." Now it was my turn to pinch the bridge of my nose.

"But I can get them shipped here."

"You know what?" I said, kind of flinching and kind of shaking my head simultaneously. I hoped I wasn't developing a nervous tick, although I suppose it wouldn't be completely out of the question. "I just can't with any of this right now. I'm about as full of weird shit as I can possibly be, and the fact that you can have *the actual Ten Commandments* shipped here—"

"Overnight express." Vincent grinned.

"No less. I just—"

"I guess it's a lot to absorb."

"You can say that again."

"Like, say, trying to understand the digital world if you're a two-thousand-year-old Pictish prince?"

I blinked up at his grinning face.

"Sure, when you put it that way," I said. "Wait a minute. You read my mind, didn't you?"

Vincent smiled, then winked at me.

"Well, don't do that again. It gives you an unfair advantage."

"I have many unfair advantages," he said, still grinning.

"Would one of those advantages involve getting me a laptop, so I can teach you the ways of the modern world?"

"Certainly," he said, before summoning Rebecca to join us in his office.

TWELVE

AS IT TURNED OUT, the Wi-Fi in Vincent's office was pretty outstanding, even though it was located in the bowels of an underground cathedral.

As soon as I fired up the top-of-the-line MacBook Pro I'd ordered off the JB HiFi website—using Vincent's AMEX Centurion card, no less—I was delighted to discover I had five glorious bars of 5G. At home, I was lucky to get one-and-half bars on 4G, but only if I stood on a chair, on the third-floor balcony, in a handmade ceremonial robe, under a full moon, in September, during a leap year.

Vincent had sent Rebecca to pick up the laptop from JB's Elizabeth Street store. It was a fully loaded processing beast that set Vincent back a cool $6,800 (I may have added a new Magic keyboard, mouse and a pair of Air Pods to the order. Sorry...not sorry). By the time she got back and begrudgingly handed me all my new goodies, I was pretty much spinning on the spot. Judging by the sour look on Rebecca's face, though, I'd say she would rather have shoved bamboo under her fingernails than do something nice for me.

And boy did that put a smile on my face.

"Now, why don't you explain this security breach Sonny was telling me about," Vincent said.

"Security breach?"

"The highly sensitive information that has made its way onto the interwebs."

Good God he made me smile. For all his pomp and weirdness, he could really be cute when he wanted to be. Or in this case, when he didn't actually want to be, but was anyway.

"Why don't you take a look for yourself?" I pulled up a selection of web pages and files I'd saved to the cloud the previous night, including a crude likeness of Vincent—which was neither accurate nor flattering—from the University of Glasgow Historical Society's website, and spun the laptop around. "Tah-dah!"

Vincent peered at the screen, curious at first, then confused, finally paling after I showed him how to scroll through all the surprisingly detailed information about the organization he'd spent much of his life trying to keep secret.

"How did you find this?" he spluttered.

"Actually, it wasn't that difficult, and between you and me, for a secret organization, you're really not that secret," I said. "There's so much chatter about you guys online, I'm pretty sure you get more hits than Kylie Jenner."

"Who?"

"Kylie Jenner. She of the cosmetics and swimwear empire?"

Vincent's face remained blank.

"*Keeping Up with the Kardashians*?"

No reaction.

"Oh, come on."

"Clarissa!" Vincent's face was turning an unflattering shade of red, and his eyes, well his eyes were alternating between shades of crimson and fiery gold, which I had come to learn was not a portent of good things to come.

"You're right, sorry," I conceded. "So, there's a lot of information out there on a number of different sites."

"Sites?"

I gave him the abridged, Cliff Notes version overview of the digital world: paranormal chat rooms and groups, and a bunch of horror reenactment groups—secret societies and what not.

"Why would anyone want to pretend to be a vampire?" Vincent asked, referring to The Masquerade, a vampire role play group I'd discovered on Facebook.

I shrugged. "You can blame Anne Rice for that."

"I've heard of her," Vincent said. "She published those diaries."

"Don't tell me they were real. Lestat isn't still wandering around New Orleans, is he?"

"No. He's fictional."

"Good to know." I nodded. "Anyway, as I see it, you'll probably want to address the sheer volume of information about the Patrons that's out there, first. Although, personally, I wouldn't be too worried about it. Far as I can tell, most of it's rubbish. Unless paranormal creatures really *do* run every Fortune 500 company, sporting team, religion and political party in the history of everything, ever. Oh, and you *really* are Jesus. Not the second coming of Jesus, mind you. I mean, *actual* Jesus" I paused. "Wait, you're not actual Jesus, are you?"

"No." Vincent shook his head. "But the other things, there is much truth to that."

Now it was my turn to gape. "I beg your pardon?"

"You heard me."

"Yes, but I don't believe you."

"Because?"

"Oh, come in. It's just so far-fetched."

"Is it really?"

"Ah, *yeah*."

"So is it easier to believe that for the entire history of the world, humans have been so intrinsically cruel and fundamentally flawed that their sole *raison d'être* has been to destroy each other? *Or* is it easier to believe that paranormal creatures have infiltrated key aspects of society, manipulating people to do their bidding for their own amusement?"

Vincent stared at me while I took the time to frame my response, because between you and me: Mind. Blown.

"Well?" he asked.

"Neither option sounds particularly appealing."

Vincent shook his head. "And yet, one of them is true."

God, I hated all this Inner World stuff. It was just so icky.

"So, what I'm hearing is that werewolves and vampires and demons and whatever else, rule the world and have done since the dawn of time?"

Part of me wanted Vincent to scoff and tell me I'd misinterpreted the situation; that I'd completely misunderstood him...or that I was at least having some kind of auditory hallucination. That would have been nice.

Of course, none of those things happened. In fact, Vincent just nodded. "Yes. Pretty much."

Hm. "So, Hitler was...?"

"A demon, obviously."

"Obviously," I said. "And Mary I of England?"

"A witch."

Made sense.

"Stalin?" I asked. "Don't tell me—um, vampire?"

"No, troll."

I should've guessed.

"Napoleon?"

"Elf."

"Cleopatra?"

"Succubus."

I marveled at the absurdity and simplicity of Vincent's revelation.

And I also had to give props to the online POO geeks for accumulating so much information about a super-secret organization without their even knowing about it. The sheer determination and volume of work needed to sift through all the tales of the supernatural and figure out fact from fiction was mind boggling. Not to mention the danger they put themselves in just to dig down and get to the truth. It was quite impressive, in a sad, my only friends have avatars, kind of way.

Not that they would have realized they were in danger.

Or did they?

That's when that curious thought I'd had previously popped back into my head. What if it wasn't about clever detective work? What if the information was being leaked? By an insider? I hadn't given the idea much weight before, but I now was really beginning to wonder if the POOs had themselves a double agent?

"Something wrong?" Vincent asked, and I blinked up at him. "You seemed to go somewhere else there for a minute."

I tapped the side of my head. "Just processing all the new info."

No way was I going to tell him I suspected there was a spy in his midst. I'd keep that nugget to myself until I could either prove, disprove it, or use it to my advantage. For all I knew, Vincent could be the double agent and spilling my beans to him could result in a swift and painful decapitation.

"So," I said, bringing the conversation back on track. "Literally, all the megalomaniacal crazies that have ever ruled faith, commerce or industry, have all been monsters? Pol Pot. Genghis Khan. Bin Laden. Caligula. Rasputin. *Everyone?*"

He tapped the side of his nose. "Now you're getting it."

This whole situation kept getting weirder and weirder.

Vincent turned his attention back to the laptop, falling into the scroll-hole I'd dug for him, devouring the information I'd unearthed about his precious, and not-so-super-secret, Patrons. When it became clear he was going to be Alicing his way around the internet for a while, I decided to check my socials, and plucked my phone from my bag.

That was one good thing about my line of work, I could do it anywhere, anytime.

"How could this happen? Is it something I did?" Vincent said, sinking back into his throne and covering his face with his hands.

"What do you mean?" I asked, finally putting my phone down. I really wasn't in the mood to deal with work.

"Did I do something to cause all this?" he asked, waving his hand to the laptop.

"You mean other than being obtuse and supremely arrogant?"

Vincent glared at me. "What's that supposed to mean?"

"Exactly what I said. You let your own prejudices and ingrained bigotry about the human race get the better of you."

"Clarissa."

"Don't, *Clarissa*, me. You absolutely convinced yourself humans were too stupid and too self-absorbed to ever suspect supernatural activity was taking place right under their noses, and you chose to completely ignore the impact information technology has had on society."

Vincent frowned. "Must you?"

"Well, it's true, isn't it?"

"Not exactly."

"Oh, rubbish. That's exactly what happened and you know it. You just don't want to admit it because it means you were wrong—"

"No."

"Yes."

"This cannot be happening," Vincent groaned.

"Oh, but it can," I replied. "And it is."

Vincent, and his band of supernatural whateverthehelltheyweres had clearly spent centuries with their heads buried in the proverbial sand, like the paranormal ostriches they were, and completely underestimated people.

Big mistake.

Humans are resourceful and clever. We explore and question things, challenge the status quo. We aren't simply lemmings who blindly believe every single thing we're told.

Okay, so maybe some of us are lemmings. I'd been guilty of believing the odd salacious rumor or two purely because I'd read it on *TMZ*. I'd also fallen for some blindingly obvious click bait, and for a while, I thought I was in an online relationship with Sam Heughan who it turns out was really a 300lb female wrestler from Taiwan named Yi-chun.

But that didn't mean everyone was as naïve as me.

"I guess we lowly humans aren't as dim as you think we are," I said with a tight grin.

"I *am* human," Vincent snapped.

"Yeah, if you're human, I'm Mary Poppins. Listen, maybe once upon a time you were human. And maybe you could also control the masses with cover ups, rhetoric and lies, but not anymore. The internet has changed all that. I want to know the mating habits of a housefly, I google it. I want instructions on how to rebuild a 1940s washing machine, I go to YouTube. I want to know if my neighbor is a blood sucking vampire—"

"I get the picture."

"Good, because right now, we have all the technology and the resources we could ever need to solve pretty much any mystery the universe throws at us...except for figuring out the Colonel's eleven secret herbs and spices, apparently," I said. "You're just lucky you haven't been publicly outed on like *HuffPost*, or something, because you know this whole shit show is just a reality series just begging to happen."

"This is terrible." Vincent stood and stalked from behind his desk. "An absolute catastrophe."

"No, an earthquake that kills tens of thousands of people is a catastrophe," I said. "Floods, wildfires, wars—these are catastrophes. People speculating about whether they saw a werewolf or an angry Pomeranian last full moon, doesn't even come close to being a catastrophe."

Vincent spun around, strode toward me, yanked me out of my chair and grabbed me by the shoulders. "Clarissa, you don't seem to understand."

Okaaaaay. Someone was freaking out a wee bit.

"The veil between the human and the paranormal world is extremely fragile. Our peaceful coexistence is precarious at best. If certain species, werewolves, vampires, gargoyles, fae...if they think, even for a split second, that humans know of their existence..." Vincent released my shoulders, ran his hands through his hair and blew out a heavy breath. "Well, there's a very good chance we could be facing an uprising."

"Uprising? Where are we, 17th century France? Are we storming the Bastille?" I said, wriggling free from his hold.

"Don't be glib, Clarissa. The Patrons keep the balance—"

"I know. You've already told me all this."

"Yes, but you didn't exactly believe me."

"And lucky for you, hardly anyone else does, either. Despite all the information to the contrary, most people don't believe in monsters or ghosts or secret societies. So, even though your secret is out—way out—it's still as safe as ever."

"I wish I could believe that," he said.

"Believe it."

Vincent looked at me skeptically.

"You know," I said, the first flicker of a brilliant idea blooming in my head. "If you want to get on the front foot with all this stuff, maybe we could use technology and human curiosity to your advantage. I could help."

"And how might you do that?"

"Well, I could set you up on a couple of social channels; a website, Facebook, Insta, TikTok. You're okay with lip syncing to 90s R'n'B tunes, yeah?"

"No," he said. "That's out of the question."

"I was joking about the lip syncing."

"I mean no to all of it. No social media or website or anything. In fact, I need to talk to my counterparts in the other quadrants and devise a plan to erase all this information."

"From what, the internet?" I snorted. "Good luck with that."

"There must be a way."

"Nope. Once it's out there, it's out there. The only chance you have of getting ahead of this is to get online and change the narrative yourself."

"I beg your pardon?"

"Change the narrative. Set up your own platforms, generate your own content. Only then would you stand any chance of regaining some control of the conversation—and I use the term *control* loosely, because let's face it, control no longer exists." I shrugged.

Vincent didn't even try to disguise the startled look on his face.

"What?" I asked.

He smiled. "You are quite the surprise package, Miss Hunt."

I shrugged again, not really knowing what to do with that.

"You know what?" I said, snapping my fingers. "You might even be able to leverage off some of the existing groups and get them to gather intel for you."

"You're joking, right?"

"Not at all. We can totally steer people away from the super-critical, top-secret stuff and get them to focus on other, less important things, instead."

"And you think this is possible?"

"Oh, definitely. Assuming you have some trivial information you're willing to make public."

Vincent's brow creased. "Trivial?"

"You know, something small you'd be willing to sacrifice for the greater good. You gotta give a little to get a little, Vinnie."

He glowered at me.

"—cent," I corrected. "Vinnnni-cent."

He shook his head. "No."

"Geez, you could at least pretend to humor me but, whatever." I closed the laptop. "Your loss. You just keep doing it your way. I mean, we've seen how well that's worked for you, so far."

I stood, gathered up all my goodies and slung my bag over my shoulder. "I'll see ya round, then," I said, heading for the door.

"Clarissa, wait," Vincent said. "Stop."

Hook.

Line.

Sinker.

I paused at the door, and turned to face him. "Yes?"

"How can you be so certain this plan of yours would work?" he asked.

"Because, it happens all the time."

Vincent snorted. "I find that hard to believe."

"It's true. It's called the Dead Cat Strategy."

"Wasn't that a Robin Williams movie?"

"Oh, FFS."

"Kidding." Vincent grinned.

"*Now* you develop a sense of humor? When I'm trying to be serious?"

He shrugged.

"Look, it's really no different than when a magician uses sleight of hand to deflect attention."

Vincent stared at me.

"Okay, let's say you're at a dinner party and the conversation is getting heated—one too many cabernets and the next thing, everyone's arguing about religion or politics or whatever. You want to avoid the carnage, so you change the subject."

"By throwing a dead cat on the table?"

"Metaphorically speaking, yes."

"And why would we do that?"

"Because then everyone would start talking about the cat."

More blank staring.

"Urgh. They'll be talking about the thing you want them to talk about, and not whatever it was that caused the brouhaha in the first place."

Vincent's eyes grew wide and his mouth popped open. "That's... That's..."

"Despicable? Diabolical? Yes, I know."

"Genius," Vincent said.

"I'll pretend you didn't say that."

"No, I meant genius in a bad way, of course."

"You're a shit liar," I said. "But I think I know what you're saying."

I returned to my chair, and gave Vincent a bit of time to get a handle on what I'd just told him. No point in pushing my point. He was 2,000 years old. He was beyond manipulating.

"So, you think you can do this? Because I'm not about to throw away centuries of work that has ensured our absolute anonymity."

"Ah, newsflash, bud: not so anonymous." I pointed at the MacBook.

"Yes, but by going public, we're really going out on a limb."

"Look, at the end of the day, you have to do what you think is right. I'm not going to try and persuade you to do anything you're not comfortable with."

Of course, I was lying. I was already mentally putting together a digital content plan and visualizing design concepts for the new POO socials—starting with changing that acronym

—because let's face it, I could do whatever the hell I wanted online and these clowns would have no idea. "Just remember," I continued. "All the chatter, the gossip and rumors, all that info about you, this organization, the inner world, and all that you stand for, that's out there—it's happening right now. It's not like if you ignore it, it'll simply go away." I tapped the laptop, for dramatic effect. "The only difference now is that you're not part of that conversation, and if you have no part in it, how can you possibly attempt to control it?" I smiled. "But, it's up to you to choose whether you want to join in or not."

I smiled smugly, chuffed at myself for making such a strong case to drag the POOs into the twenty-first century, albeit kicking and screaming. I knew Vincent and Sonny were doing whatever they could to get to the bottom of my predicament, it was the least I could do to help them with theirs.

"You know I despise your Earth logic, right?" Vincent said eventually, smiling.

I smiled back. "I know the feeling."

THIRTEEN

"WHATCHA DOIN'?" Poppy asked, hovering over my shoulder while I unpacked my new laptop and all its various accoutrements. Vincent bought me and set it up on the kitchen table. "Oooh, new toys," she added, peering at the shiny casing. "Santa visited early this year."

"Aren't you a little old to believe in Santa?" I asked, then paused. "Wait, Santa isn't really real, is he?"

"Do you really want to know?"

I thought about it and shook my head. "You know what? No. I don't. My world is batshit crazy enough as it is. I don't need any new information clogging up my brain."

"Wise decision," she replied. "What are we doing, anyway?"

"Research." I plugged in the forty-nine-inch, ultra-wide monitor I'd bought for myself for Christmas and fired up the laptop. It beeped and whirred to life and in no time, connected to the hotspot on my phone, a small miracle considering it usually took me eight years to remember the damn Wi-Fi password. "I'm trying to gather as much information as I can about the Patrons so I can pull together a digital content plan that'll—what are you doing?"

Poppy took a short break from shoveling salsa into her mouth like she was stoking the boilers on the Titanic, and grinned. "I'n habbing a fnack," she replied.

"Well, stop it. It's very annoying."

Poppy tossed the bag of Doritos she'd been hoeing into on the kitchen counter and flopped down on the kitchen chair next to me.

Who knew ghosts ate so much, or at all?

"So, can I help?" Poppy asked, pointing to the laptop. She'd pretty much polished off the Doritos and salsa I'd been saving for Tequila Thursday.

Mental note: buy more snacks.

"Sure. You can start by getting your grubby, nacho cheese hands away from my new rig."

"They're not that bad," she said, waving her orange-tipped fingers at me. "Come on, let me—"

"Not until you wash your hands and stop sprinkling Dorito crumbs around like faerie dust."

She admired her fingertips and nodded. "Fair call," she said, shoving her thumb into her mouth and sucking off the concentrated flavoring. "Mmmm."

"Gross," I mumbled and forced myself to look back at the screen and clicked the dreaded TOR browser app—a one-way ticket to the dark web.

Being on the dark web was like wading through the bowels of hell, if hell was filled with drug dealers, and sex traffickers, serial killer appreciation sites and—*wait*. It was *exactly* like the bowels of hell. Level nine.

I know, on the surface, the dark web might sound intriguing, or exciting, or maybe even a little bit thrilling (in an odd, creepy kind of way) to some. Let me assure you, once you're on there, it's anything but.

The dark web is a dangerous, disturbing, and disgusting place, filled with unimaginable horrors and a whole lotta weirdos. It's a haven for every shady criminal in the known universe to deal in every nefarious, utterly heinous activity imaginable.

? Wanna hire a hitman? Visit the dark web.

? Want stolen credit card numbers, drugs, guns or stolen goods? You guessed it, the dark web has it all.

? Interested in procuring a cursed amulet from the tomb of an ancient Egyptian princess?

You get the picture.

If it's questionable, illegal, or even the slightest bit dodgy, you can find it with a few strokes of your keyboard.

Truth be told, no one really polices the dark web.

On the dark web, no one judges you, or censors you, or beats you to a pulp with a bicycle pump because you're a despicable pervert. On the dark web, no one can hear you scream. By the same token, if you get yourself in trouble in the dark web, ain't no one coming to help you.

If it wasn't a matter of life and death, *my* life and death more specifically, I wouldn't be caught anywhere near the dark web or the creepazoids who frequent it.

But it was the only place I knew for sure I could find the real dirt on the POOs. The basic Wikipedia information I'd shown Sonny and Vincent was just that: basic. It had been a nice start, but barely scratched the surface. There were many more deep, dark POO secrets circulating out there (side note: NEVER type POO into DuckduckGo because, wowsers, you'll be exposed to a whole bunch of stuff you can never unsee, no matter how much vodka you drink), which meant the dark web was exactly where I needed to be.

Bored, Poppy eventually retreated to the lounge with Miss Miranda in tow, jonesing to watch one of her mind-numbing reality TV shows. For someone who'd died before the cast of

Geordie Shore were even twinkles in their daddies' eyes, she sure had embraced the reality genre with great fervor.

Sure, I'd been known to indulge in a bit of *Catfish* in my time—especially on those days when I needed to feel especially good about my life—but I drew the line at *Beauty and the Geek* or *The Hills* or *Love Island*. Even I had my limits.

My mobile rang, the image of my grinning father flashing on my screen in time with his designated ringtone, *Daddy Cool* by Boney M. A strange choice, some might say, but there was something about the funky 70s disco track that brought a smile to my face and put a spring in my step, just like Dad did.

"Hey, Daddy," I said, after tapping the green answer button. "What's up?"

There was a lot of noise in the background, murmurs and announcements about getting cards ready, which I took to mean he was at the country club. Of course he was. It was Tuesday. Bingo night.

"Nothing's up," he replied, cheerily. "Just thought I'd say hello and invite you over this week. We haven't seen much of you lately and wanted to know you're doing okay."

"I know. I'm sorry. That's my fault. I've just been so swamped with, er, work—" I could practically feel my nose growing as I lied.

"Have you got a new boyfriend?" Dad asked. I had to hand it to my father, he was nothing if not direct.

"What? Of course not."

"Are you sure?"

"Am I sure I don't have a boyfriend? Ah, yeah. Why?"

"I just thought maybe you'd met someone and that's why you hadn't picked up the phone."

Oh, if only it were that simple.

"Sorry to disappoint, but, nope, there is no new boyfriend."

Why did Sonny's face flash through my mind when I said that? He wasn't my boyfriend. He wasn't even boyfriend material. He was barely friend material. Yet there he was, all beautiful and perfect and sexy, filling up my mind's eye with his yummy goodness and boorish charm.

Boy, did I need to get a grip.

"So, what do you think?" Daddy asked, alerting me to the fact that I hadn't been paying close enough attention to what he was saying.

Shit. Bugger. Shit. Shit.

I only had two choices:

1. I could ask him to repeat himself, which sat at number two on my father's list of pet peeves and grievances (number one was telemarketers), or
2. I could bluff and hope to God that I hadn't agreed to buy into some weird pyramid scheme. I wasn't dumb enough to fall for that...again.

Option two was definitely the lesser of the two evils. Plus, I couldn't stand another of Daddy's telemarketer rants.

"Your mother's pretty keen," he added.

Well, that was a whole different box of dice. If Mum was keen, how bad could Dad's proposal be? Mum was a supremely sweet, rational woman; an honorable woman. She wouldn't make me do anything that I wouldn't or shouldn't be doing.

I decided to throw caution to the wind.

"Okay, well, sure, I guess so," I replied.

"Great, how's Sunday?"

How's Sunday for what? Brunch? A sail on his yacht? Church? What had I agreed to? "Errr..."

"Wonderful. I'll ring Ziggy and check if he and Asher are available."

What? Why would Dad need to check Asher's availability? And what did it have to do with—

"Asher's going to be so excited."

Oh, no. I'd just been duped into going on a blind date with Ziggy's middle son. Because, trust me, if I thought Ziggy was an unconscionable sleaze ball, then Asher was the creeper apple that didn't fall far from the yuck tree.

That'll teach me to zone out when my father was talking. It'll also teach me not to put any faith whatsoever in my mother. She was officially what I would refer to as a shifty bitch.

I had to think quick. "You know, that doesn't really work for me, Dad," I said, wracking my brain for a viable excuse, something that would withstand Daddy's Bullshit Meter. "I promised Drew I'd—"

"Drew's in Port Douglas with Arthur."

Of course he bloody well was.

"Why are you so fixated on setting me up with Asher? Why can't you be a normal parent and just call to check on my wellbeing?"

"What are you talking about? This has everything to do with your wellbeing. Wonderful woman like you. You should have some devoted schlub in your life who utterly adores you—"

"The truth is, I'm seeing someone, Daddy."

Honor thy mother and father.

Thou shalt not bear false witness.

I was going to hell.

"So, I don't think—"

"You just said you didn't have a boyfriend."

"Yes, I know, but—"

"You've agreed and that's that. I don't understand what the big deal is. I think if you gave it a chance, you and Asher could get along like a house on fire."

Spending any length of time with Asher made me want to set *myself* on fire.

"Be over by eleven," he continued, completely ignoring the *don't make me do this* vibe I was sending him. "Your mother will make paella. You love paella."

"I'm allergic to prawns, Dad," I replied.

"Fine. She'll make omelets. Whatever. See you Sunday," he chirped. "Love you."

He hung up before I had time to protest.

Poop.

Was hoping I'd die again before Sunday brunch inviting bad luck? Probably, but I'd take my chances.

In the meantime, I was going to do something far less disgusting than eat a meal with Mr. Ick Jr—I was going to search the dark web for black market organ smuggling and secret societies dedicated to monsters, and demons, and other dark, dastardly forces.

Fun!

FOURTEEN

"I'M NOT LEAVING UNTIL YOU TELL ME EVERYTHING."

I'd stormed into Vincent's office full of bluster and red-hot rage. I'd spent most of the previous day, and all of the night, elbow-deep in sleaze and some of the most disgusting content I never could have even imagined, trying to find as much intel as I could about the Patrons. And believe me when I tell you nothing I found, N-O-T-H-I-N-G, was good, including some seriously dubious information about the Patrons, which did not sit well.

Vincent and Sonny exchanged tentative glances, but neither said a word.

I crossed my arms. The *tap, tap, tap* of my foot on the parquet floor the only sound in Vincent's office.

"Well?" I said. "I'm waiting."

"Would you like to explain what you're talking about?" Sonny asked, also crossing his arms over his chest. I was so angry, not even his bulging biceps or the hint of chiseled pecs under his black *Bonds* t-shirt were enough to distract me. Much.

"You know exactly what I'm talking about," I said, flinging the manila folder containing page after page of information I'd uncovered. "What is the meaning of *that?*"

Vincent took the folder, opened it, and quickly flicked through the content, which consisted mainly of printed pages from chat room discussions, black market ads for vital organs, human sacrifice tributes and, yuck, blood trafficking, along with dozens of eye-witness accounts of the high and mighty Patrons of Order trafficking in body parts, orchestrating contract killing, and undertaking illegal organ harvesting. It was too horrifying even for me to process.

Vincent closed the folder and slid it to Sonny, who also examined its contents.

"Where did you find this?" Sonny asked.

"Where do you think?" I spat. "Were you ever planning on telling me?"

"We told you what you needed to know," Vincent said, neatly folding his hands on the desk in front of him. He was expressionless and I had to resist the urge to leap over and slap the passive look right off his face.

"Do you know just how big of a jackass you sound like right now? What I needed to know...according to *who?*"

"According to Patron laws."

"Screw the Patrons and screw your stupid laws. You're going to tell me everything and tell me now!"

My voice and demeanor were at fever-pitch and I think both Vincent and Sonny knew I'd reached my limit.

"Fine," Vincent said. "We haven't been completely honest with you."

"Well, there's a shock."

"Want me to muzzle her?" Sonny asked, thumbing in my direction.

"You could try," I replied and felt a teeny jolt of electricity skitter down my spine as the warm sound of his voice reverberated through Vincent's office.

Damn that man.

"That won't be necessary," Vincent said, lifting his hand and gesturing to the round meeting table on the opposite side of the office. "I'm sure we can all sit down like adults and have a civil conversation about this."

"I wouldn't bank on it," Sonny said, sliding out one of the heavy mahogany chairs and plonking himself down on it. His frame looked disproportionately large against the elegant Regency table.

Vincent joined Sonny and gestured for me to sit, too. I obliged, but only because I wanted to hear the full, disgusting story straight from the horses' lying, deceitful mouths.

"In 1954," Vincent said, "Joseph Murray conducted the first successful human organ transplant; a twin-to-twin, live kidney procedure. He received the Nobel Prize in Medicine for that piece of work."

"Okay." I nodded.

"Subsequent transplant procedures took place in '59 and '60, fraternal twins and siblings, respectively. By the mid-60s, they had successfully transplanted a liver and a heart, opening a world of possibilities for seriously ill people." Vincent leaned back in his chair. "Improved quality of life, prolonged life expectancy—"

"Just let me stop you there," I said, raising my hand. "If this is like the History of Modern Medicine 101, forget it, because, I failed biology and—"

"Do you want to know the whole truth or not?" Vincent asked.

I studied him closely and nodded. "Fine," I replied. "But this better be going somewhere fast."

"Maybe, if just this once you'd shut your mouth—"

Vincent shot Sonny a glare so intense, so withering, it silenced the strapping Peacekeeper in an instant.

Well, well, well, now wasn't that a nifty little trick? I needed to get Vincent to teach me that one. You just never knew when you might need to stop a certain someone's incessant yammering (said the incessant yammerer).

"As I was saying," Vincent continued. "The mid-60s saw huge advancements in transplant treatment. However, it also brought up a number of serious questions about *blah, blah, blah, blaaaaah*—"

I listened to Vincent drone on about the complexities surrounding the legal definitions of "death" and 'consent' and the ethical implications of harvesting viable organs from living and nonliving donors. He even explained how some faith-based groups originally considered organ transplantation to be a form of desecration…*zzzZZZZZZZzzzZZZZZZ*.

If I hadn't already been angry enough to kill the pair of them, I was headed that way quickly.

Vincent was getting all animated and excited, explaining the intricacies of ethics and politics around organ donation. His cheeks flushed and he spoke a mile a minute. Dead giveaway.

I, on the other hand, wanted to stick knitting needles in my ears just so I wouldn't have to listen to him drone on anymore.

"These first successful transplants were real game changers," Vincent continued. "Despite the associated medical and ethical challenges."

As Vincent continued to ramble on, not surprisingly, my mind wandered, and I started contemplating the most painful, humiliating ways I could kill Vincent and Sonny:

- lock them in my Uncle Julian's hen house and leave them to get pecked to death by his prized Silver Spangled Hamburg chickens
- push them in front of the rotor blades of a helicopter
- force feed them poisonous lizards
- throw them into an acid bath

"Anyway." Vincent cleared his throat, I assume because he sensed my waning interest and increasing ire. "When I said the transplants were game changers, I meant for humans."

"Well, yeah," I said, fighting the urge to say, *duhhhh*.

"Because they weren't exactly new for us."

I blinked, then frowned.

"The Patrons had been exploring organ transplantation for, well, centuries, even having developed a program of... Let's call them, clinical trials."

"What kind of clinical trials?" I asked with a sinking feeling in my stomach. This conversation was leading somewhere icky, I just knew it.

"For a new biological weapon," Vincent said.

"You mean like anthrax?"

Please let it be anthrax.

"Not anthrax."

Bugger.

I leaned toward him. "What then?"

"A weapon that would enable us to continue peacekeeping in a way that minimized large-scale human casualties but maximized our capacity to effectively contain paranormal outbreaks and infestations in unauthorized environments."

I glared at Vincent. "Could you be any vaguer?"

Sonny chuckled. "Is that even a word?"

"Of course it's a word, you ignoramus," I snapped, secretly hoping it actually *was* a word because honestly, I wasn't certain. I had a propensity for making things up from time to time—words, facts, and statistics, anything to help me make a point. This could easily have been one of those times.

"Now, shut up," I continued. "While Vinnie the POO over here speeds up his looooong and very boring story and gets to the actual good bits. And by good, I mean the bits that pertain to *ME*."

Sonny's eyes practically bulged out of his head and I realized that I may have just found Vincent's limit with the whole Vinnie the POO crack.

Fortunately, I was beyond caring at that point.

"Medical history is not boring," Vincent said, indignant. "It's fascinating and—"

I mock yawned. "So sleepy," I said, tapping my hand in front of my open mouth. "I can practically feel myself slipping into a coma—"

"Do I really have to spell it out for you?" Vincent snapped.

"Looks like," Sonny said. "She's just not getting it."

I glared at him. "Well, maybe *she* would get it if *someone* actually got to the point of *his* story instead of beating around the bush with all *his* useless, um, beating around the bush."

"You have quite the way with words, Hunt," Sonny said.

"Yeah, well I've got two words for you, Sonny: get fuc—"

"That's enough," Vincent snapped. He was using his angry voice.

"At least I use my words," I grumbled, turning back to Vincent. "Just get to whatever point you're meandering toward please."

"Transplants, Clarissa," Vincent said. "Interspecies organ transplants."

I scowled at Vincent, then at Sonny, then back at Vincent again. "Wait. You put monster bits into humans...on *purpose?*" My voice went super high and mega whiny.

Sonny and Vincent merely nodded.

"Are you *CRAZY?*" I shrieked, higher and whinier than before. (Mental note: make an appointment with a speech therapist, because I was likely going to rupture a vocal cord or something if I kept all this shrieking up. Plus, dogs had started following me home, which was making Miss Miranda even more disagreeable than usual.)

"You can't just go around mixing and matching body parts

from different species, you know that, right? I mean, why would you even do that? *Why?*"

"Clarissa," Vincent said in that oh-so-soothing, *let's keep Clarissa calm* voice I was quickly beginning to dislike. "Let's try and keep an open—"

"Who do you think you are, even? Frankensteining organs like some mad scientist."

"I know *that's* not a word," Sonny said.

"Scientist?" I sniped.

"No, Frankensteining," Sonny said.

I rolled my eyes.

"Actually, he wasn't mad at all," Vincent said. "He was quite a visionary, well ahead of his time. A genius, some might say."

"Who?" I looked at Sonny and pointed at Vincent. "Who is he talking about?"

"Victor Frankenstein," Sonny replied.

"Yeah, right," I snorted.

"Of course, everything changed after that wretched woman published that ridiculous biography."

"What woman?" I asked Vincent, confused and a little tetchy.

"The English lass."

For the second time in as many minutes, my brows shot up. If I wasn't careful, they'd disappear into my hairline altogether and I'd either have to have them surgically relocated or get new ones tattooed on.

"He isn't talking about Mary Shelley, is he?" I asked.

"Oh, but he is." Sonny nodded.

"You're telling me Victor Frankenstein was a *real* person? And he what, pilfered corpses and transplanted their vital organs into unsuspecting people for the Patrons?"

"In its most simplistic form, yes," Vincent said.

"So, Frankenstein's monster was what, a failed experiment?"

"No. The monster was an unauthorized side project. When

the Patrons discovered its existence, Frankenstein was stood down and the monster...terminated."

What in the hell kind of insanity had I gotten involved in?

"Why would you even do this?"

"Imagine, for a moment, a hybrid race. One with the empathy and moral compass of a human, but with the supernatural power and intuition of paranormal creatures. Imagine a world where police had super speed, strength, and split-second reaction times. Or military personnel who couldn't be killed or had accelerated healing powers. Or doctors with heightened senses and ability to diagnose and treat acute illness intuitively, with complete accuracy. It would change the face of, well, everything."

I felt a *but* coming on.

"But—"

I knew it.

Vincent hesitated. "Truth be told, we didn't completely understand how serious the ramifications of the trials could be."

"Or more likely you didn't care," I sniped.

Vincent sighed. "That's unfair and also untrue. We had some of the best clinical minds of the time working on this project, and yet, not one of them could have predicted..." He sighed heavily. "We had no idea what we would produce."

"And what did you produce?" I asked.

Sonny dropped his eyes, while Vincent's drifted skyward.

"Well?"

"The results were varied and...honestly, devastating," Vincent continued.

I huffed at him. "I swear, if you don't start giving me some straight answers, I won't be held responsible for what I do to both of you."

A smile quirked the corner of Vincent's mouth.

"And don't be laughing at me, because I'm pretty sure I

could tear at least one of your heads off before the other could stop me."

"She probably could," Sonny said, crossing his arms over his magnificent chest. "She's turning into quite the killer."

Vincent nodded. "Monsters," he said. "We created monsters of the worst kind. The first trials—"

"Experiments. Let's call them what they were, shall we?"

Vincent paused. "Alright then, the experiments didn't exactly go to plan. They were abject failures. Every single transplant recipient died within seventy-two hours of surgery."

"Rejection?"

"Along with infection and a few other complications. So, we revised our methodology, fine-tuned our techniques," Vincent continued. "We developed highly sensitive equipment, engaged new surgeons—"

"Better surgical assistants," Sonny added with a nod. "Better anesthetists, nursing and after-care specialists; each of whom was better qualified to deal with the complexities of matching and splicing human with paranormal DNA."

"And? Did it work?" I might have been angry, but I was also curious.

"In a way," Vincent said. "While the subsequent experiments did not result in any of the previous complications, some new ones emerged."

"Such as?"

"Well, for one thing we realized we had to be far more discerning about the people we chose to be the recipients of the transplanted organs."

"You're doing that whole vague thing again," I said, wagging my finger at Vincent.

He nodded. "Due to the nature of the program, we couldn't exactly conduct experiments on average citizens, could we?"

"Okay," I replied. "So, and believe me when I tell you I wish

I didn't have to ask this, who did you conduct the experiments on?"

Vincent looked at Sonny, who was doing this weird fidgety thing with the zipper on his leather jacket and nodded. "Go ahead."

Sonny took a long breath. "We made deals with certain institutions, ones that would provide a steady supply of program participants, in exchange for...compensation," he said.

"What kind of institutions?" I asked, regretting the question before it even left my mouth.

"Mainly private mental health facilities, sanatoriums..." There was a long pause. "State penitentiaries."

I gaped at him. "You're joking, right?"

Sonny shook his head.

"You paid corrupt bureaucrats to persuade disturbed people and *criminals* to volunteer to be part of experimental interspecies organ transplants?"

There was a looooong, uncomfortable silence.

"*Wellll?*" I snapped.

"Our interpretation of volunteer probably differs somewhat from yours," Vincent said, lacing his fingers together.

Differs? What in the hell did that mean? Differs in what way? I mean, persuade means persuade, unless—*wait!* The breath caught in my throat. "They didn't know, did they? The participants had no idea what was going to happen to them?"

"Technically, no," Sonny replied.

I had to swallow a couple of times to stop myself from tossing my cookies all over Vincent's handcrafted, and no doubt expensive, mahogany table. "Well, that's just...just... I want to say despicable, but I don't think it's harsh enough."

I buried my hands in my hair and was pretty sure I had the super-crazy eyes going on.

Sonny had stopped fidgeting with his jacket and was now crossing and uncrossing his legs incessantly. It was all I could do to stop myself from tearing one off and beating him over the head with it.

"Just so I'm clear on this," I said, trying desperately to regain my composure. "These volunteers…" yes, I used air quotes. "… had no idea what was going to happen to them. They were just fed some bullshit story, and next thing, they're the proud owner of a vampire liver, or elf pancreas, or werewolf he—"

I froze.

Both Vincent and Sonny blanched and grew very still, as if they were afraid to make any sudden moves that might incite me to lunge at them or rip out their spleens.

Well, playing statue wasn't working because I was totally freaking the hell out! "You?" I spat, choking back tears. "*You* did this to me?" I pointed to the center of my chest.

Their silence was deafening and was all the confirmation I needed.

I surged to my feet and slammed my palms against the table-top. It cracked down the center and splintered, sending fragments of wood flying like missiles. "*ANSWER ME!*"

Vincent also rose to his feet, albeit slowly. "Clarissa, it's not what you think."

"No, I'm pretty sure it's exactly what I think."

"Let me explain. The experiments, we stopped them. We stopped them the moment we realized—"

"*Nooo!*" I bellowed, the office walls shaking with my rage. "I will not just stand here and listen to any more of your lies."

Sonny reached over and placed his hand on my forearm. "Clarissa."

I jerked away and took two uneasy steps backward. "Don't you touch me. Never touch me again."

"Please." Sonny's voice was low and gentle. My heart suddenly ached for what might have been, for the relationship we might have had, for friendships lost. "If you just give Vincent a chance, he'll explain—"

"Ohhhh, I don't think so. You've had so many opportunities to *explain* what you did to me."

"We didn't do anything to you," Vincent insisted. "I give you my word—"

I threw my head back and laughed, it was a hollow and humorless sound that echoed through the office. "Your *word*? Like that means something?"

Vincent flinched and I knew I'd dealt his pride a savage blow.

Good.

"You've been lying to me this whole time. You let me think all this was some great mystery. You put my life in danger *repeatedly*, you played me for a fool, and now you don't even have the decency to own up to what you've done."

I was hyperventilating, but I didn't care. "You just... You just..." There was no stopping the tears, and quite frankly I didn't have the energy to even try. "I've been so scared. So confused, and it's all because of *you*. You made me believe I could trust you—"

"You can," Sonny said.

"*Liar*! You're both liars."

"Clarissa, you have to take a deep breath and listen," Vincent placated.

"I don't have to do anything you tell me to," I snarled. "All I want to know is what did I ever do to you?"

"Nothing. That's what I'm trying to tell you. We had nothing to do with—"

"I'm not a bad person. I'm not an asshole. I obey the rules and try to be good. I was just a sick, scared kid. Why did you do this to me?"

"We developed the project that was the catalyst for the experiments, but we stopped the moment we discovered what we'd done."

"You know what? If you're going to keep lying to me, I'm not going to stick around. I deserve better than this."

I hurriedly collected my belongings, stumbling in my haste and blinded by my tears.

"Clarissa, please," Vincent said.

"No!" I said. "Don't you dare say my name like that. Like you care about me. Never say my name again, period. In fact, never contact me again. Don't think about me. Don't look for me. Pretend I'm dead because that's what the two of you are to me." I took a deep, steadying breath. "*Dead.*"

I slammed the office door behind me and I'm pretty sure it came off one of its hinges.

Good. I hoped the whole damn cathedral collapsed on them.

FIFTEEN

WHO DOESN'T LOVE an unannounced visit from a stranger at 10:30 on a Thursday night?

Me, that's who.

I'd just sagged into bed, bag of Cheetos in hand, latest season of *Cobra Kai* queued on Apple TV, and Miss Miranda curled into a cute ball of floof next to me, when the front doorbell ring-a-ding-dinged like Quasimodo himself was hanging off the bell rope.

As was typical, Miss Miranda opened one eye and shot me her patented, *aren't you going to do something about that?* look, which normally had me scurrying off to right whatever perceived wrong had raised her hackles. Not this time though. This time I was cozy and comfy, and wanted to get out of bed about as much as I wanted to pull a clump of matted hair out of a clogged shower drain—you know, the yucky ones that smell like unwashed sports socks and month-old Gorgonzola.

Barf.

Miss Miranda bleated at me, and stretched out her back legs.

"Shhh..." I whispered, scratching her on the rump. "Maybe if we ignore them, whoever it is will go away?"

Miss Miranda opened her other eye when the doorbell rang again.

"Fine," I huffed, putting down the Cheetos, pausing Johnny Lawrence just as he took his first swig of Coors for the ep, and threw back the bedcovers. "I swear if it's another hawker, we're moving."

I pressed the camera button on the security panel mounted on the bedroom wall and peered at the grainy display. My bedroom was all the way up on the third floor and buggered if I was going to trudge down two flights of stairs just to be accosted by some backpacker trying to convince me to change my electricity provider.

"I doubt it'd be a door-to-door salesperson at this time of night," Poppy said, gliding into my room with a tub of Ben and Jerry's in one hand, a dessert spoon in the other. For a non-corporeal entity, she sure could pack away the junk food.

"*You* go answer the door then," I said, still trying to figure out who the hell had rung the bell. All I could see on the monitor were murky shadows and blurry outlines.

"Given only you and Azrael can see me, that'd be pretty pointless," she said.

I was still squinting at the screen, trying to decide if the shadowy figure was a human or some new-fangled beastie I hadn't yet encountered. "This is no use," I huffed, throwing my hands in the air. "I can't tell who the hell that is."

"You know if you upgraded your security system..."

"I don't need a new security system. This one is fine."

"Yes, I can see how *fine* it is. You can't even tell if that's one of the neighbors or a werewolf," Poppy said.

"I'm my experience, werewolves don't ring the bell."

"In that case, it's probably a neighbor."

The bell ring-a-ding-dinged again.

"An impatient neighbor."

I pushed the intercom button. "Yes?"

The speaker crackled and hissed momentarily before emitting an ear-splitting screech not dissimilar to when you scrape a knife along a dinner plate. It was enough to make my teeth fall out just thinking about it. Poppy may have had a point about needing a new security system. One that didn't render me deaf or toothless every time I used it would probably be a good start.

"Miss <static>? Clari<static> Hunt? My name is <static>. I really <static> talk to <static>."

"Who did you say you were?"

"<Static>cent sent me. I need to <statiiiiiiic>."

I looked at Poppy, who shrugged. "Don't look at me. I have no idea."

I sighed heavily and pressed the intercom button. "Did you say Vincent sent you?" I said into speaker. "Because I think I made myself perfectly clear—"

"Please. <Static> urgent."

"What do you think?" I asked Poppy, who'd not only made herself at home on my bed, but was now flicking her way through all my streaming services. Miss Miranda was making herself equally comfortable with Poppy's ice cream, practically burying her head in the tub. She had melty Salted Caramel Crunch *everywhere*; all over her nose, hanging off her whiskers, covering her ears. She'd be cleaning that mess up for hours.

"And stop doing that." I pointed at the TV. "I'm watching *Cobra Kai* tonight. You can watch your reality crap some other time."

"I think you need to worry more about who's at the door, and less about Netflix," Poppy said. "Sounds pretty urgent."

"Urgent. Smurgent," I grumbled and pressed the intercom button again. "Okay, hang on a minute. I'm coming down."

As I headed out of my room, I heard the *MAFS* opening

credits blare from the TV. "We are not watching that!" I called back, even though I knew Poppy wasn't listening.

When I reached the front door and peered through the peep-hole, I was surprised to see a small, spindly looking woman wearing a lime-green *Massimo* hoodie, black leggings and camo crocs (= classy) standing under my portico.

"Hello?"

"Miss Hunt, my name is Lee Picking. I must speak to you. It's urgent."

"What kind of urgent?" I asked.

"I'm sorry?"

"What kind of urgent? Why are you here?"

"Vincent sent me."

"If it's that urgent, why didn't Vincent send himself?"

"Well, um." There was a brief pause. "He's quite busy at the moment and—"

"Bullshit. He didn't come because he knows if he shows his face here, I'd rip his ears off and shove them up his..." I took a very deep, cleansing breath. "Never mind. Let's not get into that. He's too busy, so what, he sent you?" I asked, not entirely convinced this doyenne of fashion was legit. I'd become quite distrusting of late—little wonder—and my spidey senses were constantly tingling.

"I'm one of his personal messengers," Lee added.

I snorted. "He can't pick up a phone like a normal person? Send a text?" I smelled a rat. Not an actual rat this time. This time I smelled vinegar and *Blood and Bone*. Deceit. Lots and lots of deceit.

"You know, sending a personal messenger is exactly the kind of thing Vincent would do," Poppy said, poofing out of nowhere. This, of course, made me shriek and spin around like a top.

"Jeeeeez!" I said, clenching my fist and shaking it at her. "I swear, one day I'm going to clock you so hard."

"You're always so jumpy," Poppy replied, with a scowl.

"Do you *blame* me?"

Poppy rolled her eyes. "And dramatic."

"Miss Hunt? Is everything alright in there?" Lee asked through the locked front door.

"Yes. Everything's fine." I reached out and swatted at Poppy, swishing back and forth until her ghostly form dissolved into wispy tendrils before completely disappearing. "And don't come back until I tell you to," I whisper-yelled.

"I beg your pardon?" Lee asked.

"Nothing. I wasn't talking to you."

"I thought I heard a scream."

I rested my forehead against the door. "What do you want?"

"To talk to you. You're in danger."

"Vincent needs to start singing a different tune," I replied. "Because I've heard this one before. According to him, I'm always in danger."

"But you really are."

"And who put me in all this danger in the first place? Did he happen to mention *that*?"

"Er... I'm not sure I—"

"Did he tell you how I was leading a perfectly normal, respectable life until he screwed it up, and now I'm in some kind of Clive Barker hell dimension where everyone wants to kill me?"

"He didn't exactly share—"

"Did he tell you how he lied to me? *Repeatedly*? Well, not lied exactly, but he definitely withheld information, which is the same as lying, as far as I'm concerned."

"*MISS HUNT!*" Lee shouted and I startled. "Look, I'm sorry things aren't going so well with Vincent. I don't mean to be pushy or anything."

"She sounds pretty pushy to me," Poppy said, materializing next to me again.

"What part of 'don't come back until I tell you to' did you not understand?" I growled.

"Are you going to let her in or not?" Poppy asked, gesturing at the front door.

"I'm still trying to decide."

"Pardon?" Lee asked. "I can't quite hear through the—"

"Oh, for pity's sake." I yanked the front door open, startling the Skittles out of poor old Lee. She staggered back a couple of steps and nearly toppled off the stoop, but I managed to reach out, grab her by the arm and steady her.

"You alright?" I asked. "Didn't mean to scare you."

"I'm fine," she croaked. "I'm kinda jumpy by nature."

I rolled my eyes. "I would be, too, if I worked for Vincent."

Lee straightened herself, stepped forward, but paused just outside the front door, which struck me as pretty odd. "Everything okay?" I asked, regarding her closely.

"Yes, of course," she said, looking up at the doorjamb and hesitating. "May I come in? So, we can talk privately."

Tingle. Tingle. Tingle. My spidey senses were in overdrive.

"Do I look like a fool to you?" I asked, crossing my arms.

"I beg your pardon?"

"I said," I shook my head and took a step backward, "do I look like I'm the type of idiot to fall for that old chestnut?"

"What chestnut?"

"I've seen *Fright Night*. I know not to invite anyone or *ANYTHING* into my home without knowing exactly who, or *what*, they are."

"And what exactly do you think I am?"

"Well, you're gaunt, you're pasty, your fashion sense is questionable, and you won't enter my house without an invitation. I'm guessing vampire?" I replied.

Lee recoiled and snort-laughed. "I'm not a vampire, I assure you."

"Yeah, that's what Jerry said. You know, from *Fright Night*.

And then he ended up snacking on Evil Ed and turning him into a blood-sucking freakazoid in desperate need of orthodontic work."

"Miss Hunt, I'm not a vampire. I'm just polite," she said, taking a step over the threshold and entering my home. "Thank you for—*waaaaah!*"

Grabbing Lee and shoving her face-first into the hall mirror probably wasn't the most hospitable thing to do, but it was the only way I could think to confirm whether she was a vampire or not.

For all I knew, the whole vampires-can't-enter-your-home-without-an-invitation thing might very well be bullshit. But the vampires-don't-have-reflections thing, that I knew for a fact was totally, completely, one-hundred percent true.

Right?

"What are you doing?" Lee gurgled, struggling to free herself from my perfectly executed chokehold. She didn't have a chance, of course. Her puny frame was no match for me or my werewolf strength.

"I'm checking."

"For what?"

"A reflection, which..." I peered into the mirror, "you appear to have."

I released my hold and Lee swayed from side to side while she regained her balance, and the oxygen returned to her brain.

"I told you," she said, straightening herself. "I'm not a vampire."

"Yeah, well, in my experience, paranormal creatures aren't exactly forthcoming with the facts, you know?" I said as I brushed my hand over her shoulder to remove some lint which, not surprisingly, made her flinch. "Plus, I'm getting pretty tired of being surprised by unwanted visitors in my home."

Lee paused for a moment. "Apologies."

"No need." I gestured for her to enter, and she followed me

upstairs to the kitchen. "It's not your fault. At least you're not tearing up my house or trying to disembowel me. You should have been here a couple of weeks ago. Some oversized pound puppy literally tore me and my apartment to pieces."

"Is that so?" Lee said. "There doesn't seem to be any damage. Sonny must have pulled off quite the clean-up job."

"Right? A couple of days and everything was either salvaged, repaired, or replaced, good as new. You want something to drink or would you rather get right to it?" I asked.

Lee rubbed her throat. "Actually, I wouldn't mind a cold drink," she said. "I'm a little dry after…you know, the chokehold."

"Sure," I said, motioning to one of the dining chairs and making my way into the kitchen. Poppy was in there, floating near the fridge, peering at Lee.

"I don't like it," Poppy said, a scowl marring her expression.

"Don't like what?"

"Her." She pointed at Lee. "Being here. There's something off."

"You mean other than her stellar fashion sense?" I asked, pulling two glasses from one of the overhead cupboards. "Sparkling water or orange juice?" I called out.

"She gives me the willies," Poppy said with a little shudder.

I opened the fridge and pulled an unopened bottle of San Pellegrino from the door. "Of course, she's off. She works for Vincent. He's like a giant freak-magnet."

Poppy cocked a brow.

"Not me, dufus. The other freaks," I said.

"If he's such a freak-magnet, why'd you let her into the house?"

"I don't know." I shrugged and busied myself putting ice in the glasses and cutting up a lemon. "She seems harmless enough."

I decided to put out some snacks for my guest. It was rude

not to be a gracious hostess, even if your guest did work for your arch enemy and landed on your doorstep uninvited on the first night in what seemed like forever that you actually had time to watch some TV.

I couldn't even remember the last time I'd had a good binge session.

"Um, Clarissa," Poppy said, still peering into the dining room.

"I mean, Vincent knows how pissed off I am." I poured the sparkling water over the ice and dropped in a slice of lemon.

"Clarissa," Poppy repeated.

"I doubt even he'd be dumb enough to send someone over if it wasn't really serious. Sure, he's a duplicitous a-hole, but my intuition tells me —"

"*Clarissa!*" Poppy screeched and I spun around.

"*What?*"

Poppy didn't say anything, merely pointed across the kitchen island. I followed her finger, just in time to see my late-night guest TRANSFORMING INTO A GIANT WEREWOLF in the middle of my damn dining room.

What. The. *Actual?*

"I think your intuition might be a bit off," Poppy said, dryly.

I dropped my shoulders and rolled my eyes. "So much for werewolves not ringing doorbells," I grumbled. "Shows how much I know."

I scanned my kitchen bench for a potential weapon, and quickly grabbed two knives from the block I kept next to the microwave. I brandished them like samurai swords—which might have been a little more intimidating if one wasn't a bloody *paring* knife.

S-e-r-i-o-u-s-l-y?

Why can't I ever get this shit right?

Poppy shook her head and looked at me like I was the last pitiful pine tree in the lot, the night before Christmas.

Judgy bitch.

Meanwhile, it was hard to ignore the disgusting noises Lee was making as her body buckled and bowed under the force of the transformation. Her bones cracking and breaking. Her tendons stretching and snapping. There was drool and growling and gurgling. I'd never seen or heard or smelled anything like it, ever... And I'd spent a month working on Aunty Brigit's farm, shoveling shit from the pig pens. I guess I always knew the werewolf transformation would be unpleasant, maybe even painful, but I had no idea it would be this gruesome.

"That's the nastiest thing I've ever seen," Poppy said, her face twisted into a scowl.

"What about that time you accidentally walked in on Granny M getting out of the bath?" I reminded her. "You said her butt looked like cottage cheese."

"I stand corrected," she replied, scowl deepening.

The cracking and snapping and growling and tearing continued. I wasn't sure how long the process took, but what I did know was things were going to get sticky and disgusting pretty quickly.

"I'm going to need you to get out of here," I said, wracking my brain for something, *anything*, resembling a plan or stratagem or inkling that might result in an outcome that didn't involve me dying...again.

Poppy cocked a brow. "And why would I need to get out?"

"What do you mean, *why*?" I replied, pointing at the werewolf. "Monster. Fangs. Big danger. *Grrrrr*. I don't know that I can protect the both of us."

Poppy rolled her eyes. "You do realize I'm not going to get any deader, right?"

I paused. "Good point."

"Thank you."

"Just don't get in my way, okay?"

"Whatever," she grumbled, stepping behind me. "Is this better?"

I didn't respond because the horrid crunching and snapping had stopped, replaced by the potent rhythm of the beast's heart, and the huff of its labored breathing. I spun back around to get a better look at the lycan and my stomach sank.

"Oh, for the love of... Not you again," I groaned, throwing my hands in the air.

"You two know each other?" Poppy asked.

"Unfortunately, yes. This delightful, hygienically challenged, ginger nightmare was responsible for transforming most of my furniture into kindling," I griped. "Right before she killed me."

"And does this ginger nightmare have a name?" Poppy asked.

"Beverley," I replied.

"What?" the werewolf asked.

"What?"

"You said my name."

"Oh, I was telling her," I said, thumbing at Poppy.

"Who?"

"What?" I asked.

"Who were you telling?"

"My sister."

Beverley peered around the room.

"She's not... You can't see her..." I said. "You know what? It's none of your business. What are you even doing here?"

"I came to see for myself."

"See what?"

"Do all werewolves talk in riddles?" Poppy asked.

I glared at her. "How would I know?"

"Well I figured since you're part of the gang now—"

"I'm no such thing."

"Easy. No need to get testy," Poppy replied.

Beverley was still yammering on in the background, but I

barely listened. "…and so, you can imagine my surprise when I went to collect the bounty—"

That sure got my attention, though. "Wait, did you say bounty?"

"Ooooh, a bounty," Poppy said, clapping like a four-year-old at a Wiggles concert. "How exciting."

I glared at Poppy. "Exciting? *Really?*"

"How much?" Poppy asked.

"—and I was told I wouldn't be getting paid because you weren't actually dead."

"*How. Much?*" Poppy repeated, louder.

"She can't hear you," I said.

"Who can't hear me?" Beverley asked.

"No. You," I replied, pointing the cheese knife at her. "Can't hear her," pointing the cheese knife at Poppy.

"*Who?*"

"Still my sister," I said.

Beverley growled at me.

"*How. Much. Is. The. Bounty?* Ask her already!" Poppy repeated.

"Alright! Geez," I snapped and turned back to Beverley. "My sister wants to know how much the bounty is, and who put it up."

Beverley snorted. "So she can kill you and claim it for herself? How stupid do you think I am?"

Don't say it.

Don't say it.

Don't say it.

"Want me to say it?" Poppy asked.

"I dare you."

"Two-and-a-half million," Beverley said.

"*Dollars?*"

"US dollars," she clarified.

"Who even has that kind of money?" I asked. "And why would they spend it on me?"

"Can't say I know or care. All I know is killing you is going to be so much more interesting than I thought it would." Beverley dropped her gaze and growled. "You are not what you seem, Miss Hunt."

"So I've been told."

"And there's an added bonus."

"Free set of steak knives?" I asked.

"Better. Killing you means I won't have to listen to your incessant yammering ever again. And you..." Beverley pointed in the direction she *thought* Poppy was floating. (PS: she was *waaay* off.) "I'm finding a witch doctor or something to send you back to wherever the hell you came from."

"Geez," Poppy said. "What'd we ever do to her?"

"She's just cranky," I replied. "I mean, wouldn't you be if you looked like that?"

"Looked like what?" Beverley growled.

"Well, for one, would it hurt you to make an appointment with a waxer?" I said, waggling my finger up and down in front of the beast. "To sort out this train wreck."

"Shut up! Shut. Up. Shut. *Uuuuuup!*" Beverley was practically frothing at the mouth.

I glanced at Poppy, who had a pained look on her face. "Are we sure taunting the lycan is a good idea?" she whispered.

"Probably not," I replied with a wink. "But who knows? Besides, where's your sense of adventure?"

"I lost it after I died."

Fair enough.

"I'm still not convinced," Poppy continued, frown deepening.

"In for a penny, in for a pound?" I turned back to Beverley.

Poppy rolled her eyes. "Go ahead. You may as well finish what you started."

I nodded and took a deep breath. "While we're on the subject of personal hygiene, Bev, let's not forget the breath." I screwed up my face. "Seriously, pop a mint every now and again because that's just nasty."

Beverley snapped her jaws and growled at me. "You should learn to hold your tongue, princess. Before I rip it out and eat it for a snack."

"Well there's a pleasant visual," Poppy said.

In a terrifying display of power, Beverley reared up on her hind legs, and let out a blood-curdling howl. I'd never heard anything more terrifying in my life, apart from that one time Drew dragged me to the Best of the 90s revival concert in 2012, featuring Venga Boys.

#shudder

Then, much to my shock and horror, Beverley embarked on a rampage that completely destroyed my dining room; the table, six of the eight chairs, a buffet, every window and wall within clawing distance, a very expensive Xenia Design mirror I got from Artemest, and all my favorite French Provincial crockery, cutlery, and crystal.

Turns out, taunting the lycan, big mistake, because lycans are just furry toddlers who will mess your shit up if they're having a tantrum.

I turned to Poppy. "Say, I don't suppose you've got any special powers, do you? Laser eye-rays or lightning bolts that shoot from your fingertips, maybe? Anything that might help?"

She shook her head. "Nope. Sorry."

"So, I'm on my own?"

Poppy shrugged. "Pretty much."

"Story of my damn life," I grumbled.

"Like I said, drama queen."

Beverley lumbered toward me, long tendrils of drool hanging from her jowls. Why were werewolves so slobbery and gross? Seriously. Yuck.

Knives in hand, I stalked forward, blocking Beverley's access to the kitchen. She might have torn up my dining room but buggered if she was going to lay a hand on my pantry. All my yummy goodies lived in the pantry.

There was no pomp or pretense when Beverley decided to attack, she simply crouched and sprang at me. If I hadn't been paying attention, she would have bowled me over in two seconds flat and would already be snacking on my entrails. But I was paying attention, for once, and deftly sidestepped in time to see the giant werewolf career straight through my sliding glass doors, the very ones she'd thrown me through during our first encounter.

Serves her right.

#karma

As Beverley scrambled back into the dining room, I lunged at her and buried one of the knives (not the cheese one) into the center of her back. Twisting it, hard. Sure, I knew it wouldn't kill her, but hoped it might hurt enough to throw her off her game for a few seconds, because a few seconds was all I needed.

Right on cue, Beverley reared back and roared, arms flailing as she unsuccessfully attempted to grab the knife. Given the amount of force I'd used to punch that blade through her tough hide and rock-hard muscles, I knew that sucker wasn't going anywhere, even if she could reach it, which she couldn't.

That's when I saw it, that split-second opportunity I desperately needed to give me an edge, that teeny advantage that I could capitalize on, and give myself any hope of survival.

I took off, charging at her like a very cross wombat, screaming bloody murder. I was going to get a noise complaint from the Body Corporate, for sure.

As if by magic, or divine intervention, or the power of the Force, whatever you want to call it, everything seemed to switch to slow motion. I could see everything happening around me with split-second accuracy. Vapor trails followed every move we made. It was trippy as all hell.

I lunged at Beverley, swinging a tightly clenched fist with all my might, and connected squarely with her jaw. This was closely followed by a sickening crunch, which I'm pretty sure was the sound of my fingers breaking.

Werewolf superpowers or not, that was going to smart in the morning.

My heart thundered in my chest, blood roared through my veins. Buzzed from the werewolf adrenaline and cortisol, I rushed Beverley while she was still recovering from my outstanding (if I do say so myself), albeit fortuitous (if I also say so myself) right hook.

I clambered onto one of the dining chairs that had remained intact, and mustering all the energy I had, leapt into the air, not quite *Matrix*-style, but not far off, and landed heavily on her upper back.

As hoped, the maneuver forced all the air from Beverley's lungs, and I seized the chance to clench my knees as tightly as I could around her rib cage, leaving my hands free to pummel my terrifying adversary. Suddenly, those horse riding lessons my father had forced me to take when I was a kid didn't seem like such a waste of time anymore. Sorry for giving you so much grief about them, Daddy.

"Whoop! Go, Lissy! Kick that lycan ass," Poppy hollered. Then she wolf-whistled and it was suddenly like being at a rodeo, only without the sawdust and cowboys.

Beverley swatted at me from both sides, and on the third swing, her razor-sharp talons caught my shoulder and tore flesh from the bone. I stifled a scream, and instead channeled the energy into tightening the grip of my legs and punching the back of her head.

The tighter I squeezed, the more she thrashed, flinging me from side to side like a rag doll. Enraged, Bev flung herself backward, slamming us both into what was left of the exterior wall, and trapping me between her massive body and the reinforced steel frame.

Rage and desperation exploded from my gut. I grabbed the werewolf by the scruff of the neck and yanked her head back. Taken off guard, Bev yelped, but to her credit, she kept struggling to free herself. She was nothing if not persistent.

Fisting the back of her head with one hand, and her snout with the other, I wrenched clockwise with all my might.

With a sickening yelp and a snap so loud it could have passed for a bolt of lightning striking a tree, Beverley's head swiveled around, 180 degrees, until I came face-to-face with her cold, dead eyes.

My stomach lurched as her tongue lolled out of her mouth and her pupils rolled back in her skull. Luckily, I hadn't eaten much for dinner, otherwise it all would have come right back up at that moment. *Yuck.*

With a final surge of energy, I pushed away with my legs, and ripped Beverley's head clean off her body, pulling her spine out along with it.

Beverley's limp body wobbled a bit before sagging to the floor and pooling at my feet, which is exactly when I dropped her skull like it was on fire, and barfed like that time I was in Tijuana with Drew, and we had the tequila incident.

Part of me felt disgusted at myself for taking the life of another living creature. The other part of me felt, well, euphoric because let's face it, Beverley was a menace. She was a bully and destructive and she was as ugly inside as she was outside. The world was a better place without her.

I also felt like I needed a shower, a scalp massage, and a manicure because killing stuff was exhausting, and I had werewolf yuck on my clothes, in my hair, under my fingernails. Everywhere.

I slid to the floor and Poppy dropped to her knees beside me.

"*Ho-ly shit balls*! Are you okay?" she asked, patting me down and examining my injuries, which consisted of a gaping wound in my shoulder, a broken hand, and more bruises and scrapes than I could count.

"I'm fine," I said, wiping my face with the back of my hand and noticing the smear of blood there. "My brain appears to be leaking out of my nose, but otherwise, all good."

"You were so badass!" she said. "You should have seen yourself. You ripped that bitch's head clean off like it was a Barbie doll."

I peered at her. "And ripping the heads off Barbie dolls became cool when?"

"You're a total werewolf slayer. They should make a TV show about you."

"You're funny," I said, struggling to my feet. I felt light-headed and wonky.

Poppy stood back and gave me the once-over, a crease in her brow the first sign of concern. "Um, so you seem a little... Let's just say you've looked better."

I'd felt better, too.

"I'm thinking you might need some medical care," Poppy said, dragging over a chair that had somehow [mostly] survived the fracas. She patted the seat. "Sit."

So I sat, for the longest time, vaguely aware that Poppy was still talking, but not really hearing the words. I'm also pretty sure I was in shock because I felt clammy and woozy in the tummy.

"What happens now?" Poppy asked.

I surveyed the damage. "Beats me."

"Well, we're not exactly equipped to clean this mess up," she said. "And you need a doctor." She pointed to my broken hand. "I heard your bones break all the way across in the kitchen."

"Okay, well, let's get to the hospital then. That'll be a start." Bracing myself on the back of the chair, I hoisted myself to my feet. I stood there, wobbling for a second or two before collapsing back into the chair. "Or not," I said. I could feel myself fading in and out of consciousness.

Without a moment's hesitation, Poppy hopped to her feet. "Sit tight. I'm going to get help," she said, before dissolving before my eyes, leaving only tiny puffs of pearlescent smoke and the lingering scent of jonquils in her wake.

Every inch of me ached like I'd been hit by a freight train. Sitting tight was about all I could manage at that moment.

SIXTEEN

"I STILL CAN'T BELIEVE YOU CALLED HIM," I growled, as Sonny pulled his phone from his pocket and punched a number on his speed dial. "You *traitor*."

"Oh, calm down," Poppy replied. "Who else was I going to call? It's not like I could get your local Rentokil guy to come over and dispose of a *werewolf* carcass, now could I?"

She had a point.

There was only one pest control group I knew with the ability to deal with this type of mess, and their chief exterminator was standing in my living room, talking on his phone, and scrambling my brain with all his intoxicating masculine energy. Joining him were half a dozen… I didn't even know what to call them. Gnomes maybe? Miniature trolls? Elves? All I knew was they were taking photos of structural damage, measuring everything (whatever those little fluffers were, they could float!), and were hippity-hopping around like puppies at a rave. They were rowdy and joyful and full of life. I liked them.

Which was more than I could say for Sonny. He was last

person I wanted to see at that moment, or any other moment, for that matter. Stupid, lying, sexy Sonny, with his *I'm here to protect you* bullshit, and amazing biceps, and killer smile, and tight, tight, black Levi's.

I was going to throttle Poppy. Once my hand was fixed.

Not long after she poofed out of my kitchen in search of help, Poppy poofed right back in with the burly Peacekeeper in tow. Next thing I knew, he was standing in my living room, all massive and oozing his delicious pheromones everywhere, while I tried to figure out if there was a way to kill someone who was already dead.

Beverley was on to something. I needed an exorcist. But I didn't have one handy, so instead, I told Poppy to make herself scarce before I smudged her ass with a sage stick.

She obliged, albeit reluctantly.

Clever girl.

Anyway, as far as I was concerned, this whole crappy situation was all stupid Beverley's fault. Why couldn't she have turned back into a human after she died like any ordinary, er... werewolf? A buck-toothed, knock-kneed woman weighing all of fifty kilos dripping wet would have been far easier to dispose of than 300 kilograms of matted ginger fur and general grossness.

"No, it's not a social call," Sonny said to whomever was on the other end of his phone—not that I was eavesdropping, not intentionally, at least. I mean, I couldn't *not* hear him. He was only a few feet away from me and wasn't exactly using his inside voice. Besides, we were in *my* living room and I was entitled to listen to all conversations that took place therein.

"I need a clean-up crew at the Caroline Springs address from a couple of weeks back," he said.

God, I needed to get a grip.

"One adult lycan."

Having Sonny in such close proximity was scrambling my brain...and other parts of my body.

"Breed? Um…" Sonny nudged Beverley's severed head with the toe of his black biker boots. It rolled back and forth a few times before coming to rest, face up on the tiles, staring at me with dead eyes. "*Mandrillus.*"

I had to keep reminding myself Sonny couldn't be trusted. He'd *lied* to me on so many occasions and proved over and over again that he was someone who made questionable decisions. If I couldn't trust him, I couldn't be with him; and if I couldn't be with him, then all these lusty feelings just had to disappear.

It was that simple.

"Actually, no. It's Beverley," Sonny replied.

Easy peasy.

"No, not me," he continued. "Um…a civilian."

That got my attention. So, I was a civilian now? Was this the army? I guess we were in a war of sorts.

"You can say that again." Sonny chuckled and I wondered what on earth could possibly have been sooooo funny that he would laugh while I was in the throes of an anxiety attack of monumental proportions.

I had every right to feel sorry for myself, considering what I'd been through.

My house was in shambles, *again.*

I'd had to fight a stupid werewolf to the death, *again.*

I was traumatized and bruised and broken, *again.*

And, I was really starting to wonder what the hell I'd done in a previous life to deserve all this drama, *again.* Had I been an Amway distributor or something?

I rubbed my eye with the heel of my hand—the unbroken one—and stretched, catching a whiff of myself in the process.

Yuck.

I reeked of BO—possibly mine, possibly Beverley's—and dried blood. I needed a bath, and a drink (preferably vodka), and a massage, and a holiday. Somewhere sunny…but not *with* Sonny. Sunny the adjective, not Sonny the proper noun.

I was having a full-scale meltdown, and yet, there he was, Captain Delicious, flirting and giggling up a storm with some fluffed-up floozy who no doubt was taking pot shots at my unfortunate situation — *ooooh!* I bet he was talking to that prissy bitch, Rebecca. This was exactly the type of situation she'd love; me injured, and my property reduced to little more than kindling.

I cleared my throat to get Sonny's attention and raised my rapidly swelling hand. He glanced at me, and after briefly sizing up my injury, nodded and returned to his call.

"Listen, I'll also need a medical crew at the same address. Civilian down."

What was this "civilian" talk, all of a sudden? He'd never called me that before. Was he trying to make a point about something?

Sonny made a little more chitchat that I was too preoccupied to pay attention to, before hanging up and sliding the phone into his pocket.

"And how is Rebecca?" I asked. Yes, I used a *tone*; a bitchy, slightly jealous, catlike tone I wasn't particularly proud of.

Sonny tilted his head and smiled. "She's fine," he replied. "I'll let her know you were asking after her."

"You needn't bother," I said, cradling my busted-up hand that was now throbbing like an infected molar. "What happens now?"

I knew my bottom lip was quivering and I was struggling to stop myself from blubbering all over Sonny like a big, drooly dog. But this was not the time to fall apart. This was the time for big-girl pants.

"Well, the cleaning crew will be here within the hour." He gestured at the broken furniture and bits of dead werewolf strewn around the room. "To sort out the mess."

I looked at the carnage and whimpered. "They'd better be able to get all that blood out of the upholstery," I said.

"Don't worry your pretty little head about a thing," he placated. "They'll clean everything up so it's good as new, just like last time. And after that's done, we'll sort out your neighbors."

My head snapped around so fast, I'm pretty sure I gave myself whiplash. One more thing for the medical crew to look at when they arrived. "Sort out my neighbors? What the hell does that even mean?" I said, looking Sonny in the eye.

"Well, they've seen and heard a lot of weird shit. We can't have them walking around with that kind of information, now can we?"

"So, what, you're not going to *kill them*?" I shrieked. "I mean, I know Mrs. Brady smells like camphor and birdseed, and don't get me started on Anja and her incessant Alpine yodeling," I said. "And sure, Rupert from unit fourteen keeps waaaaay too many ferrets—"

"How many is too many?"

"He's got, like, forty of them. It's disgusting."

"Okay."

"But I don't want any of them, you know." I raked my thumb across my throat. "Dead."

"What? Oh, for heaven's—" Sonny huffed, his demeanor shifting. "But that's the best part of my job, killing innocent people who just happen to be in the wrong place at the wrong time. There's nothing I enjoy more." He scowled at me. "Way to go and jump to conclusions."

He looked genuinely wounded, and for a heartbeat, I kind of felt bad for even thinking he was capable of murdering half the occupants of my townhouse complex. But, only kind of.

"Do you blame me?" I replied. "It's not like it's outside the realm of possibility, is it?"

Sonny shook his head and crouched in front of me, pinning me with his amazing emerald eyes. "I know we betrayed you... *I* betrayed you and I'm sorry for that, I really am." His voice was soft, almost lyrical. "But it had to be done. It practically killed me having to lie to you and seeing the hurt in your eyes." Sonny looked away and breathed deeply. Was he collecting himself? Was he getting choked up? If he was getting choked up, then I just knew I'd be getting choked up. I felt a lump rise in my throat.

"When will you understand, Clarissa?" Sonny took my non-broken hand and pressed his lips to the back of it. "I'd die before I let anything happen to you."

That was one big, motherfucking lump. What the hell was it? A grapefruit?

"I'm on your side, I promise. We all are."

"What about Rebecca?" I asked.

"Yeah, not her."

I felt myself smile, and some of the tension between us eased away, much to my chagrin. I wanted to stay angry at him. I *needed* to stay angry at him. Why was I not staying angry at him?

"That's better," he said, stroking my cheek. "I love it when you smile."

Gulp.

"And just for the record, when I said we'd take care of your neighbors, I meant we'd alter their memories, not kill them. It's a painless procedure involving a small dose of THC and some earth magicks."

"Oh," I said, relief washing over me. Mostly. Because if they really wanted to get rid of Anya the yodeler, I'd be happy to look the other way.

"Wait..." I frowned. "You get them high?"

"Well, yes. Point is, we don't just go around killing innocent people."

I raised a brow, and he smiled.

"Anymore. We don't kill innocent people *anymore*. And we would never... No, *I* would never, hurt you."

I cocked my head.

Sonny's smile widened. "*Again.* I'd never hurt you *again*."

I could feel the last of my resolve slipping away like so much sand through the hourglass. Not good. Sooooo not good.

"Now, why don't you let me take a look at your hand?"

"Like I'm going to let you triage my injury," I said, but there was no heat in my words. Truth be told, I didn't have the energy to be indignant. I was exhausted. I'd just have to be angry in the morning. At that moment, all I wanted was for the pain to go away, so I stretched out my arm and presented my injured hand to Sonny.

He took it in his, and examined it closely, and frowned. "We definitely need to get this seen to," he said. "Looks like you've broken a couple of bones."

No shit, Sherlock.

"Lucky you've got those new, whizz-bang werewolf healing powers, hey? Otherwise, you'd be in a cast for months with this type of break."

"Some pain killers wouldn't go astray in the interim."

There was a bit of a commotion in the front room, followed by murmurs of adulation and acknowledgement from the hippity-hoppity things. I peered past Sonny to see Vincent stepping on to the landing and into my living room, surveying the scene.

Great. The other guy I didn't want to see. My anger might have started thawing toward Sonny, but I was still harboring a bunch of cranky feelings toward Vincent. I wasn't *that* much of a pushover.

Sonny released my hand and stood. "If you don't mind…" He pointed at Vincent. "I have business to attend to."

I nodded. "Go. Do your job."

"You're more than a job, Clarissa." He smiled. "You should know that."

I watched as Sonny joined Vincent, who was being greeted by a dozen dizzy gnomes bouncing around him with unfettered glee. How did I end up with half the paranormal world in my living room? When did people stop phoning before they visited? Was I running some kind of halfway house where every freak in the universe took it upon themselves to swan in and out as they saw fit?

"Who's that?" Poppy asked, poofing back into the room, and craning her head past me.

Speaking of freaks who swanned in and out as they saw fit.

"I thought I told you to leave," I said.

"I did, but I got bored, so I'm back." She grinned. "Who's the hottie?"

I turned in the direction in which she was pointing, praying to all the deities that she wasn't talking about Sonny. I would have hated to have to wrestle Poppy over the affections of a boy, again. Last time that happened, I won. Okay, she won. It was grade six, he was Jeremy the captain of the school volleyball team, and yes, it still stung.

"Oh, that's Vincent," I replied. It was the first time I'd seen him outside his office. It was weird, like when you're at the supermarket and you see your accountant, and you can't for the life of you remember their name, or what they do, or how you even know them, despite the fact they've been all up in your financials since the dawn of time. *That* kind of weird.

"You never mentioned he was a total babe," Poppy said, nodding appreciatively.

I looked back at Vincent and shrugged. "I guess I don't look at him that way."

"Are you looking at him with your eyes open?"

"What? Of course. I look at him the way I look at Dad. He's like a father figure." Although, I did remember having the same reaction the very first time I saw him, too. Back when he was the hot stranger and I didn't know anything about werewolves, or ghosts, or what the inside of a body bag looked like.

Ahhhhh, the good old days.

"Only without the incessant lawsuits, I hope," Poppy added.

"Thank God."

"You know," Poppy said. "I'm beginning to think there are no ugly creatures in the paranormal world."

I snorted. "You've obviously never seen a troll."

"Like on Facebook?"

I sighed. "No, that's exactly the opposite of what I meant."

Vincent strode over to where we were sitting and smiled. He was wearing his signature Paul Smith trousers, a charcoal turtleneck and black leather duster. His hair was combed off his face and he had a smattering of stubble on his chiseled jaw. Poppy was right. He was a handsome man. I'd stopped noticing with all the lying and dying.

"I don't remember inviting you over," I said. I was only half-serious.

"Well, given the way you pop in and out of my office like it's a 7-11, I thought it was high time I returned the favor," Vincent replied.

Smart ass.

"And you must be Poppy," he added, not missing a beat and turning to my sister.

She smiled and nodded and blushed and, FFS, she *giggled*. God, even she was fangirling all over him.

Urgh.

"It's a pleasure," he said, extending his hand.

Ohhhh no.

I leaned into Poppy. "Just kiss it and move on," I whispered, gesturing at his hand.

Vincent stifled a laugh. "A simple shake will suffice."

I glared at him. "Oh, *now* you're okay with a shake?"

"I'm evolving."

I couldn't help but smile. "Nice."

He and Poppy shook hands, before he turned his attention back to me. "Speaking of hands, how's yours?"

I sighed. "No good. It's broken."

"We'll get that seen to, lickity split."

Lickity split? What the hell did that even mean, because I'm pretty sure the mental image I'd conjured wasn't at all what Vincent had meant. Or at least I hoped it wasn't.

Sonny placed his hand on Vincent's shoulder. "Can we talk?"

"Of course." Vincent nodded.

"Privately."

Then, they both looked at me.

"What?"

"Any chance you can make yourself scarce?" Sonny asked.

"In my own *home?*" I replied. I wouldn't have called it a screech; others might.

"If you don't mind," Vincent added.

I looked at Poppy and she sneered at me. "Not so pleasant when you're told to go away, is it?"

Why was I constantly surrounded by smart asses?

Sonny and Vincent remained stony faced.

"Fine, but I'm only going as far as the kitchen."

"Thank you," Vincent said.

"You're just lucky I'm hungry." I stood and immediately regretted it. Everything hurt, not just my hand.

———

From my vantage point near the pantry, I could see Vincent and Sonny had moved to the spot in my lounge room farthest away from the kitchen. They were speaking in super-hushed tones, which meant they *really* didn't want me to hear what they were saying, but I wasn't having any of that.

"So, what are we eating?" Poppy asked, peering into the fridge.

"We're not eating anything," I said, trying to position myself in such a way that I could see what they were doing in the lounge.

"What? But you said—"

"Will you please shoosh," I hissed, pointing at the mini-POO powwow taking place in my front room. "I'm trying to hear what they're saying."

Poppy slumped back against the bench and crossed her arms. "Fine, but I'm starving."

"You're always starving," I said before refocusing on Sonny and Vincent.

"Well, she's in there with her head twisted clean off and spinal cord ripped out," I heard Sonny whisper.

"Is that right?" Vincent replied, a little too enthusiastically. "All the way out?"

"From brain stem to coccyx." Sonny beamed, like a proud father getting the lowdown at his kid's parent-teacher interview. *Yes, Mr. Sonny, Clarissa is doing particularly well in Biology and Home Ec. She also shows great aptitude for art, creative writing, and ripping werewolves' spines out. She's still struggling with PE and French, though.*

"Interesting," Vincent said. "Which breed?"

"An adult *Mandrillus*."

"Not Beverley?"

Sonny nodded.

"Well now, that is impressive," Vincent said, turning around and sliding me a sly wink.

My guess? He knew I was listening.

"Why don't you join us, Clarissa?" he said, motioning to me. "Given you're going to eavesdrop on our conversation, privacy doesn't seem to matter."

Ha! I knew it!

"Come on," I said to Poppy, and she followed me back into the living room.

"A full-grown *Mandrillus* is a formidable adversary; strong, explosive, powerful," Vincent said after I rejoined them. "They are extremely potent fighting machines. Notoriously difficult to injure, much less kill."

I flinched at the word kill. "Can you not?" I asked. "This is not something to be proud of. This is terrible."

"Terrible? Are you kidding? This is unbelievable," Sonny said. "A *Mandrillus*, Clarissa. Big score."

I wasn't really vibing with their whole *yay, Clarissa's a murderer* stance.

"I can see how you might be feeling uneasy, Clarissa," Vincent said. "But I assure you, you have nothing to feel bad about."

Pfft. What would he know? I was a murderer, and no one seemed to care. But I cared. I cared a lot.

Sonny grinned at me with such satisfaction that I wasn't sure if I wanted to kiss or kill him.

"Look, as I see it, you've done the world a favor," Sonny said. "You're safe, the big bad wolf has been, um…deboned, and we now know you've got a bounty on your head. It's definitely win-win."

Pfft. Win-win, my butt.

"You're not the one who killed a living creature with your bare hands," I grumbled. "I don't feel like a winner. I feel like a killer."

"That beast," Sonny said, pointing to Beverley's remains, "tried, and succeeded, to kill you at least once before. She was about to do it again, and believe me, she would not have stopped until you were forever dead this time. You defended yourself, and you defended all the other innocent people she would no doubt have gone on to kill, because that's what they do. Werewolves are killing machines. Who knows how many people you've saved?"

I couldn't help but smile. "That was quite the pep talk," I said.

Sonny shrugged and it was so cute, I wanted to squish-hug him.

I'm fickle. I accept this.

"He has a way with words, don't you think?" Vincent asked. "You should listen to him. Everything he said is correct."

Sweet talkers.

"So, what happens next?" I asked.

Vincent and Sonny looked at each other, like they were trying to decide who was going to speak first.

"Hello? Next steps, what are they? Rally the troops? Batten down the hatches?"

"Actually, we think it's time we introduce you to the Patrons."

I snorted. "Yeah, right. I hope you set him straight."

When Sonny didn't respond, I immediately glared at Vincent. "He did set you straight, right?"

"If by 'set me straight', you mean agreed we should organize a supervised meeting before the end of the week, then yes, he did."

I shot them both a dirty look. "Please tell me you're kidding."

There was a lot of head shaking and mumbling, looking elsewhere and foot shuffling. For such highly regarded, powerful men, they seemed pretty nervous to me.

"Well, I won't agree to it. Both of you, *and* the Patrons, can shove it. I just won't go."

"You could do that," Sonny said.

"You can count on it."

"Orrr..."

"Or what?"

"Or you could agree to the meeting and see what the Patrons have to say about your situation."

"Why would I do that? We all know how it's going to unfold.

I'll go to the meeting, and then the first chance one of them gets, they'll rip my damn throat out and sell it on the black market."

They briefly glanced at each other. It was subtle, but I noticed it.

"No one's going to end up minced meat. I told you, I have forbidden—"

"And you really think the werewolves give a fat rat's ass about your ultimatum, Vincent? They aren't exactly the most stable of species."

Sonny snorted. "Ain't that the truth? But I don't think you quite realize the power Vincent wields over the creatures of the Inner World. It'd be a pretty brave lycan, or any other species for that matter, to cross him. He's not a man to be trifled with. What he says, goes."

"But I don't understand, why on earth would you want the Patrons to know about me?"

"Firstly, I have an inkling at least some of them know already," Vincent said. "And I want to know who, and I want to know how they found out. Secondly, as somebody once told me, if we hope to gain even the slightest semblance of control over a situation, we have to become part of the conversation, isn't that right?"

Oh, FFS. "*Now* you choose to listen to me?" I grumbled.

"Not at all." Vincent grinned. "I listened to you about the handshaking thing, too."

"Fine," I conceded. "What's the plan?"

SEVENTEEN

THERE WAS NO PLAN. Or if there was a plan, I certainly
didn't know anything about it, probably because I'd been
whacked out of my gourd on painkillers and muscle relaxants for
three days, which went kinda like this:

DAY 1

- ZZZZZZzzzzzzzzzzzzzzZZZZZZzzzzzzz
- ZZZZZZzzzzzzzzzzzzzzZZZZZZzzzzzzz
- ZZZZZZzzzzzzzzzzzzzzZZZZZZzzzzzzz

DAY 2

- ZZZZZZzzzzzzzzzzzzzzZZZZZZzzzzzzz
- Eat some toast.
- Sip some tea.
- Vomit the toast and tea back up again.

- Brush teeth.
- *ZZZZZZzzzzzzzzzzzzzzZZZZZZzzzzzzz*
- *ZZZZZZzzzzzzzzzzzzzzZZZZZZzzzzzzz*

DAY 3

- God, I'm starving. I also need to pee.
- Pee.
- Eat toast and keep it down.
- Sip tea and keep it down.
- Shower.
- Pee again.
- *ZZZZZZzzzzzzzzzzzzzzZZZZZZzzzzzzz*

So, it was early on day four that I found myself in Vincent's office, after swearing blue and purple that I'd never set foot in it again. Funny how your resolve crumbles when you're confronted by a 300kg werewolf in your dining room.

"Are you ready?" he asked.

I'd just found out there actually was a plan. It was a sucky plan. I didn't like it. But apparently I didn't have a say in the planning of the plan, so I just nodded.

"As ready as I'll ever be," I said with a shrug. What did I know about being ready? I was never ready for anything anymore.

Vincent flicked a switch on the old-school intercom on his desk. Who even had an intercom anymore? Come to think of it, I couldn't even remember seeing Vincent with a cell phone. Surely he had one, right?

"Can you come in here please, Rebecca?" he said into the speaker.

Great. Rebecca. She hated my guts. Admittedly, that probably had more to do with Sonny than it did with me. It was pretty obvious she wanted him all to herself, and saw me as some kind of threat. Which was ridiculous. Even if Sonny was interested in me in that way, which he wasn't, I wasn't interested in him. He was not at all my type. Who even liked rugged, sexy, hero-types, anyway? Pfft. Not me. So, her petty, passive-aggressive crap was completely misdirected.

I didn't want Sonny.

She could have him.

He was all hers.

Totally fine with me.

Totally.

Fine.

I'd have to have a word with her and give them my blessings, maybe then she'd stop sneering at me all the live-long day. Maybe I could buy her a fruit basket, or a certificate to my waxer? That might help.

I was going to kill the bitch with kindness, if it was the last thing I did.

And if that didn't work, I was just going to kill her.

There was a knock on Vincent's door and Rebecca slipped quietly into the room. "Yes, sir?" she said, nodding at Vincent and, yep, you guessed it, sneering at me.

"Please summon the Patrons for an emergency meeting on Friday."

That certainly got her attention.

Rebecca collected herself, nodded and scribbled some notes in one of those old-school shorthand pads you might see in an episode of *Mad Men*. It was like living in a time warp around there. Someone needed to get Vincent a cell phone, Rebecca a tablet...and maybe a personality transplant, just for good measure.

"Species?" she asked, without looking up from her notes.

"Lycans and sanguisuge."

"Region?"

Vincent steepled his fingers, and hummed. "Just the southern region, for now."

"Pardon my ignorance," I said and Rebecca snorted. Bitch. "Sanguisuge?"

"It's another name for vampires," Vincent said, lowering his eyes. "To be honest, it's a less-than-complimentary term. They don't really like to be referred to as such. So, I wouldn't use it when you meet them."

"Handy tip," I said, nodding. "And, what exactly does it mean?"

"Leech," Rebecca said, before casting a little disapproving side-eye my way. I wasn't about to give her the satisfaction of knowing she was rattling me like a pebble in an empty can, so I shot her my most brilliant, thousand-watt smile—the one I normally reserved exclusively for pressers and holiday selfies. If she noticed, though, she didn't react, instead returning her attention to Vincent as if I wasn't even in the room.

She didn't know it yet, but I was going to make her love me, even if it killed me...or her.

"Rank?" she repeated, and Vincent returned his attention to her.

"Invite the alphas and elders...and Seconds in Command."

"It'll be an evening meeting then? To accommodate the vampires?"

"Of course, and be sure to arrange sufficient food for them. We *do not* want a repeat of last time."

"What happened last time?" I asked.

They both looked at me and paled.

"There was an incident," Vincent said. "Very bloody. Spleens and entrails everywhere. My dry cleaning bill alone—"

I held up my hand. "That's okay, I get the picture." I glanced at Rebecca, noting the look of disgust on her face, which could have been directed at me, or the result of the discussion about the entrails. I couldn't be sure.

Then, the corners of her mouth curled into a terrifying grimace, and that's when I realized she wasn't going to order any food for the vampires at all. Nope, she was going to starve the freaks for two days and then slip them a key to my town house with an invitation to an all-you-can-eat Clarissa-shaped buffet!

Mental note: stay at Drew's on Friday night, just in case.

"Accommodation at the Mercure?" Rebecca asked Vincent.

"Yes," he replied. "Actually, no. Make it the Grand Hyatt. This is an important meeting and I need everyone refreshed and relaxed if we're to have even the slightest chance of a positive resolution."

Nothing about the conversation was filling me with any kind of confidence.

"I'll get right on this for you," Rebecca replied, closing her notepad. "Is there anything else?"

"Actually, yes. Could you bring me some tea? Earl grey, if you don't mind."

"Certainly." She nodded.

"Clarissa, would you like anything?" Vincent asked.

"Actually, I wouldn't mind a glass of—"

"I'm sure she doesn't," Rebecca said, without so much as a sideways glance. Have I mentioned that she's a complete bitch? "I'll go and make the arrangements now." And with that, she turned on her heel and exited the office without uttering another word.

"Why does she hate me so much?" I asked, turning to Vincent.

"I wouldn't say she hates you," he replied, leaning back in his chair. "She just doesn't know you very well. She takes a while to warm up to people. I'm sure once she—"

"The last time I was here, she removed all the TP from the ladies' room and locked me in a cubicle for forty minutes."

"Oh," Vincent said, disguising his giggle—badly—with a fake cough. "Well, I'm sure she didn't mean anything by it. She probably…um. You know what? I don't know why she hates you and I don't care. We have more pressing issues to discuss."

I smiled, appreciating his honesty. "Sounds ominous."

"We need to devise a way of explaining your situation to the Patrons without the whole thing turning into a diplomatic nightmare."

"Is it really such a big deal?" I asked. "I mean, it's just a little organ transplant."

"I could say no," Vincent said, and I felt a wave of relief. "But I'd be lying."

Nuts.

"Last time we faced a diplomatic issue such as this, it resulted in the Salem Witch Trials."

I flinched. "You couldn't dumb down the messaging a bit? Soften the blow, maybe?" I said, conscious that I was tapping my foot and clenching my teeth. If my hand wasn't still sore after being busted up, I'd have been twiddling my thumbs or cracking my knuckles, for certain.

"I'm not in the habit of lying," Vincent said, and I snorted.

"You disagree?" he asked, leaning farther back on his throne.

"From personal experience? Hell, yeah."

"I have never lied to you, per se."

"You haven't always been entirely truthful either, *per se.* Plus, you're the head of a super-secret organization. Your entire *raison d'etre* is predicated on your ability to lie," I said.

"Okay, then let me rephrase. I'm not in the habit of lying to my friends."

"Is that what we are?" I asked, leaning in and enjoying the way his cheeks turned slightly pink. "Friends?"

"Well, perhaps not friends. Acquaintances, maybe. Associates. I'll leave you to decide."

"I think you totally love me," I replied. "In a strictly platonic, grandpa kind of way."

He pursed his lips. "You may have grown on me."

"Really?" I smiled.

"In a platonic, grandpa kind of way."

"Then why do I feel like your pet project, half the time?"

"I know you don't see it, but I'm on your side, Clarissa. I've never meant you any harm. Neither has Sonny. He was following my orders, and I ordered him to tell you nothing."

Likely story.

"Why didn't you tell me you were behind this?" I said, pointing to my chest.

"Because I wasn't," he replied.

"See, there you go again, lying straight to my face."

I slumped back in the chair.

"But, I'm not lying. I swear," he snapped. "Yes, the Patrons initiated the original experiments, but they were shut down many decades before you were even born."

"Then, how do you explain what happened to me?"

"I can't. I don't know what happened. As far as I know, all the reports, clinical notes, diagrams, schematics—everything—were destroyed when the program ceased in 1850."

Vincent stood, walked to his drinks trolley, and poured himself a shot of something golden and aromatic. He gestured to the cut-crystal decanter.

"No, thank you," I said, waving my good hand at him.

"Someone, somehow, has come into possession of the project files," he said, returning to his chair.

"You mean the ones that were destroyed?"

He took a swig from his glass and eyed me over the rim. "Yes."

"And now you have to explain the super-secret, not to mention disastrous, Frankenstein project and the mystery of how Clarissa got her werewolf heart to the other Patrons?"

He raised his brows and nodded.

"You're in deep shit."

"Up to my eyeballs." He sighed. "But you must believe me

when I tell you, I have no intention of handing you over to them."

"Come again? Handing me over to who—"

"You are, well, you're a miracle. You shouldn't even exist," *"Handing me over to who?"*

"It's my job to ensure no harm comes to you. Everything I do, is to protect you. I just wish you'd believe me."

I paused and studied his face. He looked earnest enough. He looked like he was telling the truth. But who knew with him? I couldn't read him, not yet, anyway. He somehow scrambled my bullshit meter, which left me with many reservations.

I was left with nothing but my gut feelings. But could I even trust myself?

The pained look on Vincent's face told a very specific story, and I found my resolve wavering. I really had no choice but to trust him, despite his deception so far. He was the only one who knew about my situation, and the only one who could help me get to the bottom of it all. I had little choice.

But little choice didn't mean no choice, or that I couldn't have a little fun with him, in the meantime.

"So, what you're trying to say is, you care about me."

"In a way, I suppose—"

"I'm kind of like your bestie, aren't I?"

"I said no such thing," he replied.

"But that's what you're thinking," I jibed. "Admit it."

Vincent pursed his lips and frowned. "That's quite enough."

"Don't worry, your secret is safe with me." I nodded, then winked. "Bestie."

"Don't test me, Clarissa."

"Hey, you're the one who announced we were friends. I was just here for the icy stares from your receptionist."

"Clarissa."

"BFF."

"Keep this backchat up and I'll feed you to Rebecca," he muttered, and I laughed.

Then I stopped laughing.

"Did you say, feed me to Rebecca?" I asked.

"Indeed." He was the one grinning now.

"*Feed me to Rebecca?*" I repeated, and he nodded. "What the hell *is* she?"

EIGHTEEN

REMEMBER THAT AMAZING SCENE from the first Harry Potter movie, the one in the dining hall with the soaring ceilings and rows of tables positioned under that breathtaking canopy of delightful floating candles?

And remember how hundreds of excited Hogwarts students were seated at those tables, chattering and roughhousing while they eagerly waited for Dumbledoor to join the rest of the faculty at the huge table perched high atop the dais at the front of the hall?

And remember how when you first saw that scene, it was so magical and so wondrous you just couldn't believe someone had the creativity and imagination to think something like that up in the first place?

Yeah, well, walking into the *Magnam Triclinio*, which Vincent explained meant Grand Dining Hall in Latin, location of the emergency meeting of the Patrons of Order, was exactly like that scene…if Stephen King had written the screenplay and Wes Craven had directed it.

Sure, the room was nothing short of spectacular, with overhead twinkling lights and gold cutlery and serving ware covering the tabletops. However, instead of boisterous students, the great room was filled with every drooling, scabby, mucus-secreting, and can I add, hygienically challenged, beastie you could ever imagine... And then some.

And, of course, instead of Dumbledore, the throng was waiting for the arrival of their host, Vincent, his Chief of Security, Sonny and yep, you guessed it, the guest of honor and freak du jour, yours truly.

"Who are all these people?" I asked Sonny, while Vincent was being the dutiful host. We were standing on the side of the dais, watching, as he showed guests to their seats. "I thought this was supposed to be a small gathering."

"This is a small gathering."

"Are you kidding? There's like two hundred people out there."

"They're not exactly people," he said.

"True, the drool was a bit of a giveaway." I shuddered. "So, who are they?"

Sonny scanned the hall and pursed his lips. "Think of them as groupies."

"Groupies? Like rock stars?"

"Okay, then, think of them as members of their entourage."

"Whose entourage?" I asked.

Sonny smiled and gestured to the dignitaries making their way to their seats. "You'll see."

"Why are you always so cryptic?"

"Am I?"

"Whatever."

On the dais at the front of the grand hall was the VIP table where the most important of the important guests were being seated. Thankfully they looked human and less like they belonged in the freak exhibition at Madame Tussaud's than the rabble seated at the tables below.

You could tell the VIPs were super VIP-y by the imposing row of refrigerator-sized bodyguards lined up behind them, two of whom I'd recognized from the Royal Melbourne Hospital when I'd tried to check on Nash. Sonny explained he often employed them as protectors for night meetings, because they were all, in fact, gargoyles by day.

Apparently, you could find them perched, all stony-faced and imposing, high atop some of Melbourne's oldest and most beautiful churches and theaters from sunup to sundown. In fact, you could find them pretty much in any city in any major city in Europe, North America, and some parts of Asia.

By night, however, they roamed the streets, prowled the laneways and apparently worked as bouncers at inner-city clubs and pubs...and hospitals.

Who knew there were so many supernatural creatures right under our noses?

The more I learned about the paranormal world, the more I longed for the blissful days when I knew none of it, because, once you know, you can't unknow, you know?

The VIPs looked, well, like you or me, with not so much as an oozing pustule or stray hair between them. Thank goodness, because the thought of sharing a meal with one of the scabby freaks below made my stomach churn.

To the left, sat three verrrrrry pale people. I wouldn't quite say they were translucent, but they weren't far off. The trio consisted of a supremely elegant woman with lush, auburn hair and eyes so light they were practically white. She was flanked by two gentlemen wearing exquisite Burberry dinner suits in navy, with one sporting a vintage platinum-and-diamond beveled pearl master Rolex, that was not only rare, but cost more than my town house. There was some serious cashola sitting in those seats; and it was old money. Old, *olllllld* money.

The wealthy, pale ones sipped from solid-gold goblets and spoke to each other in hushed tones while they sized up the other creatures in the room. It didn't take a genius to work out they were vampires which probably meant those goblets weren't actually filled with wine, but more likely blood.

Human blood.

Eeeeeeyuck.

Despite their beauty and remarkable grace, I took an instant dislike to them, and felt my hackles rise at their mere presence. I couldn't ever remember having had such a visceral reaction to another person before, unless you counted Sonny, but he didn't so much make me want to rip his throat out as he made me want to rip his clothes off.

On the opposite side of the dais sat another three stylishly dressed guests whom I struggled to take my eyes off of: an older gentleman with salt-and-pepper hair, warm, golden eyes and a jawline that made me think he would have been quite the dish in his day; and a much younger woman and man flanking him.

From the moment Vincent greeted them, I felt an inexplicable pull toward the intriguing stranger and his party.

Several times, I caught him looking at me, and not the way the drooling hoards looked at me—like I was dinner—or the way Sonny looked at me—like I was dessert. When this man looked at me, he wasn't sizing me up. He was studying my face, gauging my responses, reading my emotions. There was a softness in his eyes that was absent in his counterparts, but there was pain, too, and a sense of sadness I could only liken to the loss I'd felt when Poppy died.

When I eventually caught a whiff of him, his scent reminded me of an open fire—clean, white smoke that curled around me like well-worn jammies. He smelled like old books, freshly baked Anzac biscuits, and espresso. He smelled like that old, comfy jumper you just couldn't get rid of despite having more holes than honeycomb, because you just loved tugging it on when you wanted to feel warm and safe.

I don't know why, but he smelled like home.

"And who's that?" I asked.

"Silvio De Benedetto," Sonny replied. "Werewolf alpha. That's his daughter, Donatella, and his son, Max. He's the second-line heir to the De Benedetto pack."

"Second-line?"

"Yeah, he's like the alpha lite."

"Why can I never understand what you're talking about?" I asked.

Sonny's brows shot up. "Because you rarely pay attention?"

He had a point.

Donatella and Max bore a striking resemblance, not only to each other, but to Silvio. It was obvious they were his progeny. Their eyes were also gold. Not hazel or amber, but actually gold, their hair raven. Donatella's cascaded in loose curls over her narrow shoulders and down her fully exposed, flawless back.

The stunning frock she wore reminded me of the black-and-silver Azarro cocktail dress Nicole Kidman wore to the Tribeca Film Festival in 2005. Did Nicole know how to pick a statement dress, or what? And so too did this woman, it seemed.

Max, well, he was clearly channeling his inner James Bond in his Gucci, single-breasted mohair suit, Cartier cufflinks and slicked-back hair that matched the blue-black tones of his sister's.

While their resemblance was unmistakable, their expressions differed greatly. Max looked relaxed and refreshed, completely at ease with himself and his surroundings. Donatella, on the other hand, had the most terrifying Resting Bitch Face I'd ever seen, and I'd met my fair share of primped and puckered Insta-Princesses. I'd ridden twenty-seven floors in an elevator with a certain hip-hop artist and fashion mogul in Vegas two summers earlier, for heaven's sake, and not even *he* could hold a candle to this woman's chilly, passive stare.

She was so cold, and so aloof, I felt like if I were to touch her, I'd likely turn into an ice sculpture.

"So, what did you mean by second-line?" I asked, again. "Is he not the actual heir?"

"Not exactly," Sonny replied. "Silvio's firstborn son, Dante —the rightful heir to the pack—disappeared about ten years ago."

"Disappeared?" Well, that explained the sadness I felt when I saw Silvio. "What happened to him?"

"No one knows for certain. Rumor was he fled because he couldn't deal with the responsibility of being the future alpha."

I bristled unexpectedly, surprisingly uncomfortable with the accusation. "That can't be true."

"It could be, but I doubt it. I knew Dante. He was a good man; young and inexperienced, but he had a brave heart and a sharp mind. He had the potential of being a great leader, like his father."

"What do you think happened?"

"Most likely, he was murdered by a rival pack, cut up into teeny tiny lycan bits and fed to the fishes."

Well there was a lovely image I'd never be able to unimagine.

"Why would anyone do that?"

"Not every werewolf is a fan of Silvio's leadership style. He believes in cooperation, compromise, and peaceful coexistence."

"None of those things are high on the werewolf agenda, then?"

"Ah, no. There are a lot of lycans that support a return to the old ways, when the werewolves were the dominant species."

"Dare I ask?" I said, reluctantly.

"It's exactly what you think it is; slaughtering humans— slaughtering everything really—plundering wealth, taking over land, basically ruling the Inner and Outer worlds with an iron fist. Werewolves have a propensity for mayhem and carnage, not peaceful coexistence."

"So, despite not knowing what happened to Dante, Silvio named a new heir?"

"He had to," Sonny replied. "A werewolf pack without an heir is extremely vulnerable; wide open to being overthrown, having their bloodlines severed, and all their assets and wealth stolen. It's pretty much a death warrant."

"Charming," I said.

I was conscious that I was still staring at the De Benedettos, but couldn't bring myself to look away. They were simply hypnotic, and I felt an immediate connection to all three of them. Even the cranky-looking one.

"What's with all the questions, anyway?"

"What? No, nothing. Just curious."

"Really?"

"Yes, really."

"Because if you're interested in Max…or Donni, for that matter, I could introduce you. She's single and I'd be more than happy to hold the camera if the two of you ever decided to, you know—" He winked. "Get to know each other better."

I elbowed Sonny in the solar plexus hard enough to make him double over and force the air out of his lungs with an audible *whoosh*.

"As if I'd let you film anything, you perv."

"Ah, but you *are* interested?" He wheezed, rubbing the spot where I'd jabbed him.

"That's for me to know and you to find out," I said, turning away from him.

I heard him chuckle. "Tease."

"What's so funny?" Vincent asked, joining us on the side of the dais.

"Sonny's trying to set me up with Donatella," I said.

"Really?" Vincent asked with a quirked brow. "I'm sorry. I presumed you were, you know, heterosexual. My mistake."

"Oh, I am heterosexual. Strictly a meat and two veg kind of gal," I said, and Vincent's brows furrowed. "But, if I *was* going to dip my toe in the lake of ladylove, she would totally be my type. I mean, seriously, is she a feast for the senses or what?"

"You don't think she looks a little...chilly?" Vincent asked.

"Chilly?"

"Like she has an icy pole up her bum."

I laughed so loud, quite a few guests turned and peered at me. "Where'd you even hear that?" I whispered, stifling my chuckles.

Vincent shrugged. "Around."

"Personally, I think she looks like the kind of woman who'd bite your bits off and spit them out before she tied you to a radiator and beat you with a riding crop," Sonny said, matter-of-factly.

Both Vincent and I turned and faced him.

"What?" Sonny asked. "I'm just saying she looks—"

"What the hell is wrong with you?" I asked, noticing how Vincent kept glancing over at Donatella and, if I wasn't mistaken, she was glancing right back at him. There may have even been a little blushing on his part.

Interesting.

"Something you'd like to tell me?" I asked, nudging Vincent.

"I'm sure I don't know what you're talking about."

"I bet," I replied.

"Are we ready to go?" Sonny asked, clearly deflecting. "The natives grow restless."

That's okay. Vincent and his secret crush on Donatella would keep.

Sonny nodded and rubbed his hands together with probably a little too much glee. "Sure thing, boss. Let's get this party started."

NINETEEN

EVER FEEL LIKE AN EXHIBIT AT THE ZOO with dozens of people (or non-people, in this case) gaping at you like you were a deleted scene from the Tommy Lee/Pam Anderson sex tape? That's what I felt like, seated at the center of the VIP table, Vincent to my left, Sonny to my right, and every freaky, googly-eyed weirdo in the place staring at me.

Vincent had explained my, let's call it *unusual*, situation to the lycan and vampire big-wigs, and to say they were *piiiissssed offffff* would be the biggest understatement since Jim Lovell contacted mission control and said, 'Houston, we've had a problem'.

As it turns out, Vincent's top-secret interspecies organ transplant program was so top secret, no one other than Vincent, Sonny, and a handful of medical professionals, including Victor Frankenstein, knew anything about it.

The fact the experiments had officially ceased more than a century before I was born, much less before I'd received my transplant, didn't go over that well with the POOs either, because it meant someone had not only found the original project brief and research results that had supposedly been destroyed in the 1800s, but had also resumed the clandestine experiments without anyone (meaning Vincent) knowing.

If the reactions of the esteemed guests were anything to go by, it was quite a problem, and while Vincent did his best to field the barrage of questions the VIPs fired at him, his responses only seemed to enrage them further.

And let me tell you, enraged vamps, and werewolves—not pretty. There were flashing fangs and gnashing teeth, growling— lots of growling—there was an inordinate amount of hot, stale breath and slobber e-v-e-r-y-w-h-e-r-e. It was very much a duck-and-cover situation. Only there was nowhere to duck and I was pretty sure Sonny was the only one who had me covered; and Vincent, of course, but he was pretty busy and I knew Sonny had the goods to protect me.

"How the hell did this happen, *Vincent?*" Donatella raged. "This is outrageous!"

"At least we can agree on that," the female vampire, whose name I found out was Beatrix, fired back. She was basically the vampire second in command, but from what I understood, she called most of the shots because the vampire, errr, boss? King? Emperor? I had no idea how the head of the vampires should be addressed—let's just call him the oldest bloodsucker at the table —was more interested in scrolling his mobile phone than repre-senting his minions.

Vampires were strange creatures. It was little wonder no one liked them.

"Well, that's a first," Sonny muttered. "I didn't think I'd ever see the day when lycan alphas and vampire elders agreed on anything."

Mental note: the vampire big-wigs are called elders.

"Check me out," I replied. "Bringing immortal enemies together like the Paranormal UN." I tried to keep my tone light, but I just didn't have the energy to fake my usual level of enthusiasm. I'm the first to admit I use humor as a defense mechanism at stressful times, but this wasn't your ordinary, run-of-the-mill stressful time. This was like the most mega of mega stressful times in the history of stressful times, and my reserves were totally depleted. "They could probably use my diplomatic skills in Europe or the Middle East."

"So, what does this mean for us?" Beatrix snapped. "Can you guarantee news of this won't get out to the humans?"

I rolled my eyes. "Oh please, like we'd broadcast this shit show to the world," I grumbled. "That wouldn't make us look crazy at all."

Beatrix bared her fangs and slid me the saltiest side-eye I'd ever seen. "Shut your mongrel up, Vincent," she spat. "Or I'll shut it up for you."

Um, what now? Did she call me a mongrel?

"More importantly," Donatella continued. "What do we do about it?"

It? What, it? Did she mean me? Was she calling me, IT?

"I know I speak for the packs of all four regions when I say we will not tolerate some *bitser* muddying up our pristine bloodlines."

"Listen carefully," I growled. "If one more of you freaks calls me it or mongrel or bitser or whatever, I'll—"

"You'll what?" Felipe, the vampire elder asked, managing to drag his attention away from his phone long enough to glare at me. I couldn't be sure, but I took a stab and guessed he was probably trolling Vamp Tinder, scoping his next ménage a lunch. "What exactly is it you think you're going to do against the likes of us?"

Ire, red hot and raw bubbled up from my core, burning the base of my throat. It was so potent, so vile, I almost choked on it. "You wanna see what I can do, you smarmy—"

Vincent flashed me a look that screamed *SHUT UP!* There

was desperation in his expression I couldn't remember having seen before. It was sobering and made me realize things might just be a teensy bit more serious than I'd understood them to be. So, I took stock of the situation.

There were three werewolves and three vampires seated at the table on the dais, and God knows how many in the great hall. I had no idea whose side the gargoyles were on (whichever issued the biggest pay checks, I presumed) which left only Vincent and Sonny on #teamclarissa. Given the extent to which I was outnumbered, and the chances of me actually reaching Felipe in time to pummel him before one of the uber-freaks gutted me like a fish, were pretty slim. So, I decided to shut my mouth, swallow my pride and leave my *fightin' words* unspoken.

Begrudgingly.

I might have been angry, but I wasn't stupid.

As Sonny had implied, Silvio was the biggest of the lycan big-wigs. As alpha of the De Benedetto pack, the most powerful across all four regions, he was revered and respected by *most* of the lycans; feared and admired by other paranormal species. And apparently the humans thought he was a stand-up guy, too. He'd received an Australia Day Honor in 2019 for his philanthropic activities and support of indigenous education programs. Of course, HRH Queen Elizabeth II might have reconsidered her decision, if she actually had known Silvio was a werewolf, but as it stood, she had thought he was a neat guy. Then it occurred to me, maybe she had known that Silvio was a werewolf. Vincent did say most world leaders were actually from the Inner World. I made a mental note: ask what species the British royal family are.

For being such an important player in the Inner World, Silvio remained conspicuously silent for most of the meeting. Donatella, though, was a completely different story. Not only would she not shut up, but she only seemed to get angrier and screechier the more the conversation progressed. In fact, I was pretty sure she was the main reason a [mostly] civil-ish meeting was descending into an all-out screaming match.

"Can you guarantee nothing like this will happen again?" Filipe, he who I planned to kill in the not-so-distant future, asked before taking a giant gulp from his blood-filled chalice. A dribble of syrupy, ruby liquid trickled from the corner of his mouth, which he proceeded to lick clean with a disturbingly long, and unusually pointed tongue.

I knew he was putting on a show for my benefit. Was that supposed to be frightening? Alluring? Sexy? Was that it? Was he trying to seduce me? God, he wasn't trying to flirt with me, was he?

Because if he was, yuck.

The only thing he'd succeeded in doing, was making my stomach churn. It took all my willpower not to barf my dinner up in the breadbasket in front of me.

"Because this is completely unacceptable," he continued. "We, the vampires of the *région sud*, demand an immediate review of how this travesty transpired. We also expect a comprehensive report detailing how you plan to deal with this…this…" Felipe pointed at me with his pallid, limp-wristed hand. "Abomination."

"Seriously?" I muttered. "*Abomination*? Why don't you just shut your cake hole, you prissy, pinch-faced pillock?"

I looked up and all eyes in the room were on me.

Gulp.

Vincent squeezed my shoulder, hard. "Shoosh," he hissed. "I'm not kidding."

I slumped back in my chair and crossed my arms over my chest. I may even have pouted.

Shooshing wasn't exactly my strong point. Neither was patience, diplomacy, or tact. I guess they were skills I'd have to learn quick smart, or I'd be lunch meat.

Sonny leaned toward me. "Your big mouth is making this so

much harder than it has to be. So, shut it before I shut it for you."
His teeth were clenched, and he was pretty much growling at me,
rather than speaking.

"Pardon?" I asked, not sure I'd heard him right.

"You heard me. Shut. Up. I'm sick and tired of your
mouthing off and then having to clean up your messes all the
damn time. You're exhausting. Just, for once, do as you're told."

Where in the hell had that come from? Sure, I knew I could
be a bit blabber-mouthy. Lord knew it had gotten me in trouble
more than once, but was this really the time for Sonny to bring
that up?

Sonny glared at me. "And stop gaping at me like that," he
snapped. "You look like a damn fool."

Whoa.

He pointed down the table. "Just pay attention to what's
going on and stop flapping your yap. I won't tell you again."

Sonny wasn't exactly using his inside voice, and he'd drawn
the attention of pretty much everyone in the hall, but especially
everyone seated on the dais. They were regarding him with
macabre interest, like they could sense something was brewing.
Unfortunately, I could sense it, too.

"Tell me, Vincent." Silvio surprised everyone by breaking his
silence. His timing was impeccable, defusing the escalating
tension in a microsecond (and not a microsecond too soon, from
where I was sitting). He spoke with a prominent Italian accent,
and a low, authoritative tone I found oddly soothing. "The heart
she has…whom did it belong to?"

Vincent looked at Silvio, his face devoid of emotion.

"Was it one of my *branco*, my pack, who died, so this…"
Silvio sighed. "*Scusa*, I want to choose my words more carefully
than my daughter and your other guests." He paused and
regarded me closely. "Who died so this creature lives?"

I could live with creature. At least it wasn't insulting.

Despite my unfortunate situation, Silvio seemed more

reasonable than the others seated at the table, including Sonny, who was still brooding like a toddler.

Silvio was more reserved; his temperament even, and his general demeanor poised. What was it with this guy? What was it about him that made me feel so calm and safe? Was it because we had the werewolf connection going on? I mean, it would explain why I'd taken an instant dislike to the bloodsuckers when I saw them (although, from what I could gather, they weren't exactly popular with any of the Inner World folk). So, it made sense that it gave me some subliminal connection to the lycans.

Maybe?

The other thing I found curious was that Silvio didn't at all come across as the violent, cruel, and impulsive monster I imagined a werewolf alpha would be. He was more like my grandpa, only he didn't smell of mothballs and menthol cigarettes.

Donatella, on the other hand, was a shrew, and Max, well, he reminded me of cotton candy. You're only interested in it because it looks nice, and ten minutes later, you can't even remember what it tasted like.

Vincent sighed. "I'm afraid that's something we don't know as yet, *Alto Re*."

Apparently, *Alto Re* means king or your royal-awesomeness —something like that—in Latin. It's how alpha werewolves are addressed, or so Sonny told me.

"Well, I say this is completely unacceptable," Donatella snapped, slamming her palm against the table, rattling the cutlery and sending condiments and breadsticks flying.

"Of course you would," I grumbled, hoping no one else would hear me. Judging by the lack of reaction, no one did.

I wondered how two people who were so different could possibly be related to each other, much be less father and daughter. Where Silvio was even-tempered and rational, Donatella was screechy and erratic. Where Silvio was polite and diplomatic, Donatella was like a petulant adolescent with all her ranting and raving. I half-expected her to scream her little lungs out, stamp her little feet, and storm off to her room at any moment.

Silvio oozed class and the kind of elegance that only came from good breeding and good lineage.

Donatella was like the runt of the litter. I didn't like her. I mean, not as much as I didn't like the vampires, but I did find myself wishing one of the gargoyle/bouncer/bodyguards would step up and clip her upside the head and smack some sense into the little turd. None of them did, of course. So, I had to settle for fantasizing about how one day, I'd rip the skin off her face and turn it into a bum bag.

"If you can't control what goes on within this organization, Vincent, I'm sure we can find someone who can."

I could practically see the steam billowing from Vincent's ears. "I'll remind you who you're speaking to, *Donatella*," Vincent shot back. "You may be the daughter of the alpha, but I have been the head of this organization for millennia. Longer than you or any of your bloodline have been alive. I've seen more alphas come and go than you've had manicures. You would do well to speak to me in a manner fitting my station."

"And I'll remind you," Donatella sneered. "That your position as head of this organization is predicated on your ability to maintain absolute discretion and secrecy. I don't think anyone here can honestly say that's been the case of late. Is there anyone else we can blame for that?"

Silvio scowled at his daughter, and in turn, Sonny scowled at me. What was his problem, and what the hell had I done to piss him off? It's not like I'd asked the surgeons to transplant a werewolf heart into me. It's not like I was the one who'd posted all that info about the POOs on the internet. In fact, if it wasn't for me, they wouldn't even know any of that even existed. I'd even committed to helping them clean the damn mess up. I didn't deserve greasy looks from Sonny or anyone else. I deserved a bloody medal!

Silvio said nothing, of course, but I could tell he was annoyed at his daughter by the way his nostrils flared, and his brows furrowed. And the fact that he smelled like angry—sour milk and bitumen.

Sonny pretty much had the same expression on his face, because clearly, he thought I was responsible for the mess we'd found ourselves in. I don't know how, though. Okay, so I may have killed stinky Beverley, and yes, I did die and come back to life a lot. And sure, I did shoot out the back of a hearse and get myself arrested. And I may have told Nash the whole story about the POOs. Where was I even going with this?

"You've put us in an extremely vulnerable situation, Vincent. Unsanctioned, interspecies organ transplants; humans rising from the dead—"

"Just one human," Vincent corrected.

"That's one too many," Beatrix replied.

She and Donatella must have both graduated dux from the same School of Bitch.

"Local police being alerted to paranormal phenomena. Hospital staff witnessing resurrections. Private properties being destroyed—"

"In Vincent's defense, werewolves caused most of that damage," I said. "I believe that's on you."

"What the hell did I tell you?" Sonny said. He'd completely abandoned his inside voice and I knew that more, if not all, eyes in the room were on us again.

"I assure you," Silvio said. "It wasn't any member of my pack who attacked you. We are still investigating—"

"If it were one of ours," Donatella sneered. "You would be dead by now and we wouldn't even be having this discussion."

Boy, I was getting so, so tired of that little smarmy cow.

"*Zita!*" Silvio barked. "*Basta.* That's enough."

Apparently, Silvio was getting tired of her, too.

Good for him.

Everyone at the table snickered, except Vincent, Sonny, and me. We all seemed to have lost our senses of humor.

"We have it under control," Vincent said, his tone even as ever. I knew he was faking, though, because he smelled like stress sweat and stale beer.

"Do you really? Because I don't see how," Donatella growled. "What I do see is a colossal disaster that requires immediate and radical attention."

I wondered exactly what Donatella meant by radical attention. It's not like they could un-transplant my heart, could they? Not without killing me at least.

A tiny shiver skittered up my spine as I realized that's *exactly* what Donatella wanted. She wanted someone to tear my werewolf heart clean out of my chest and kill me! Well, now I didn't feel half as bad for wanting to rip her face off.

"On behalf of the *mort-vivant*," (that's French for vampire, according to Sonny). "I can confirm we agree wholeheartedly with the lycan position," Beatrix said. "I say we fix the problem here and now. I say we rid ourselves of this abomination and be done with it." She punctuated the last three words with short, sharp taps on the heavy wooden table. "Then we find out who is responsible for this, and get rid of them, too."

Melodramatic much?

"What you say is not relevant, Bea." Vincent said. "You'll do well to keep your opinions to yourself."

"I will do no such thing," she replied. "I have every right to—"

Vincent rose to his feet so quickly, I didn't even realize he'd moved until his chair toppled backward and clattered against the marble floor. When he slammed his palms on the table, I nearly jumped clean out of my skin and the rest of the great hall fell eerily quiet.

"Silence! I've had about enough of this—"

"No," Sonny said, rising from his chair, too. "Let her speak."

Um, what now?

Vincent turned and glared at his 2IC. Their eyes locked but the humor and affection they normally shared was completely gone, replaced with... What the hell was that? Anger? Resentment? Disgust?

"Sonny, stand down," Vincent growled.

"No."

"Stand down before I make you stand down." Vincent was also speaking through gritted teeth, which wasn't typical of the way he spoke to Sonny. It was more like the way he spoke to me, but only when he was super, super angry. Which had been a lot.

"You could try," Sonny replied, squaring his shoulders.

What the hell was going on? Why were Vincent and Sonny at loggerheads? Had Sonny lost his ever-loving mind?

"Do you have something to say to me?" Vincent asked, straightening and expanding his chest.

"Only something I wish I'd said weeks ago," Sonny replied.

Vincent raised his brows and for a moment, I thought he was going to lash out at Sonny. He didn't, of course. He had too much self-control for that.

"Very well," he said, extending his arms. "Go ahead. Please enlighten me."

"Do I have to spell it out for you? We've spent weeks running around cleaning up all the ridiculous messes this woman has caused." Sonny pointed at me. "We've had to pay off so many people, help witnesses *forget* the things they'd seen because of her careless attitude. She's a menace and I just don't understand why you're continuing to protect her."

What the hell was going on?

"With every moment she's alive, all we've ever worked for is in jeopardy."

"Finally, someone's talking sense," Donatella said.

"All the sacrifices we've made, all the people who have given their lives… Has it all been for nothing?"

Sonny yanked me to my feet and dragged me closer to him. "She doesn't care about us or the work we do."

Well, that wasn't *entirely* true.

"She isn't interested in this organization or the Inner World. And why would she be? She's not one of us. She never will be. She hates us. She said as much herself."

When did I say that? Recently? I was having trouble thinking of an example.

"She's nothing more than a spoiled, self-centered brat who only cares about herself."

"I beg your *pardon*?" I snapped.

"Shut up," Sonny said. "For once just shut your mouth."

"Sonny!" Vincent's eyes had turned a deep crimson and were narrowed on his chief Peacemaker. "Release Miss Hunt and return to your seat."

"No," Sonny repeated. "You've clearly lost all control of this situation, and I, for one, will not allow one stupid mistake to ruin everything we've worked for centuries to build."

Oh, hello confusion. How nice of you to join us.

I couldn't even begin to understand what Sonny was getting at. Why was he saying all these horrible things? Why was he gripping my arm so tightly? I was pretty sure I was going to have a hand-sized bruise on my bicep for the next month, just to add to the broken metacarpals in my hand and the sixty stitches in my shoulder. I just didn't understand where it was all coming from. I mean, I knew I hadn't always acted responsibly, particularly in relation to the low profile the Patrons liked to maintain. And sure, I could be a little impulsive and maybe I'd gotten myself into situations that others probably wouldn't. But I never wanted or intended to ruin anything. Maybe I hadn't understood the importance of everything from the get-go, nor did I take it seriously, or care much about… Where was I going with this?

Oh, yes, despite my flaws—my very *human* and very *justifiable* flaws—did I really deserve all this animosity from one of the only people I thought was on my side?

A sense of doom began coiling through my body, like that time with Nash in the records room. And we all remember how well that turned out.

Vincent looked furious. "So, you choose this particular moment to share your concerns with me? Now, rather than, say, in private, so we weren't forced to air our dirty laundry in front of our guests?"

"It's not like you would listen to me, is it? You're so wrapped up in protecting Clarissa, you've neglected to protect the only things that matter—the Patrons and the Inner World."

I tried to yank my arm from Sonny's vise-like grip, but to no avail. The more I tugged, the tighter he squeezed.

The air in the great hall crackled with tension, and I mean that *literally*. Tiny silver, onyx, and garnet sparks of pent-up energy zig-zagged, snapped, and swirled above Vincent and Sonny like microscopic demonic fireflies.

Sonny's breathing had become disturbingly labored, like he was fighting to keep his emotions in check. Either that or he was having an asthma attack, and as far as I knew, he wasn't asthmatic.

His scent had completely changed, too. Gone was the intoxicating aroma of rain and peaches that normally emanated from his body, replaced with a complex, dense stench that reminded me of burning rubber and AV Gas, with sub-notes of rotting flesh and WD40. The air was thick with it, and I found myself struggling to catch my breath.

Panic. Attack. Immanent.

"Vincent, I have dedicated my life to you," Sonny said. "I have followed your orders without question, with utter devotion. I've lied for you. I've killed for you. But this time, I just don't understand."

The blood roaring in my ears was so loud and so fierce, I could hardly hear myself think, much less keep up with what was going on at the table.

"Sonny, I'm warning you," Vincent growled.

"You can warn me all you like, Vincent, but I'm no longer prepared to listen."

"So, it's treason then?"

"Never," Sonny said. "My job is to protect you, protect this organization, and protect the human race. I'm a Peacekeeper, for heaven's sake."

"I'm not feeling very peaceful right now," I said.

Sonny didn't speak to me, but squeezed my arm so tightly, I actually thought he might break it. "Please," I whimpered. "Sonny, you're really hurting me."

His eyes flickered to mine, and I desperately searched them for even the smallest hint of the softness or compassion I knew he was capable of. I saw none of it. I saw only bitterness and hatred and anger.

He looked back at Vincent. "You might not be able to see what's happening right under your nose, but I can."

I looked at the Patrons seated at the table and was horrified to see the bloodlust in all their eyes. Everyone but Silvio, who remained stoic and quiet.

"Sonny! I won't say it again. Stand down!" Vincent yelled.

"No. A thousand years of dedicated service and you're willing to throw it all away because of this." Sonny shook me like I was a rag doll, and to my horror, I heard the sickening crack as my humerus snapped under the pressure of his grip.

I cried out, but nobody listened. Nobody cared. Tears rolled down my cheeks and I felt fear, real fear, for the first time since I'd gotten mixed up with the Patrons and their terrifying world.

"Well, I won't let you," Sonny continued. "I pledged my allegiance to this organization, to you, and sometimes that means I have to help you when you can't help yourself,"

I didn't see the silver dagger Sonny pulled from the pocket of his long, black coat, but boy, I sure as hell felt it when he plunged the ten-inch blade to the hilt into my back, and straight through my heart.

He then braced himself, and with a sadistic growl I thought was only reserved for truly evil paranormals, twisted the blade with all his might.

I heard Vincent scream, his heart-wrenching, *"Noooooo!"* echoing through the great hall.

For a split second, everything came into sharp focus—the ferrous smell of blood, MY blood, pulsing from the wounds in my back and chest. I could clearly see the tip of the blade that protruded from my chest, and heard the wild howls and piercing screeches of both the werewolves and the vampires as they cheered and applauded Sonny.

I felt the silver blade sizzle and fizz in my chest, as my werewolf heart struggled to reject the poisonous metal. The pain was paralyzing, unbearable, and all consuming. I'd never felt anything like it before and prayed I'd never experience anything like it again... Assuming I had an *again* to experience.

With the silver blade still shish-kabobbing my heart, I could feel myself slipping into the terrifying, inky darkness of death. Peace lay in its velvety embrace. Peace and stillness and love.

And Poppy.

I closed my eyes and struggled to focus and ignore the pain. Someone was at my side then, someone familiar, someone who loved me. They cradled my body, held me close and murmured softly in my ear, and although the words were unintelligible, the sound of their voice gave me comfort. I slowly opened my eyes and saw Azrael, his eyes fixed on mine, his lips moving as he whispered the words I couldn't understand.

Confusion slammed into me.

Holy shit, I was actually dying—for real, this time. Why else would Azrael have been there? He was a Reaper, and he was clearly…reaping.

Tears streamed down his face and onto mine. His grief was strangely comforting. Knowing someone who really cared about me would be there for my final breath gave me strength.

It made me sad, though, realizing it was all over. My life, that is. There were so many things I still wanted to do. I hadn't learned to surf or seen the Northern Lights. I'd never even done Kokoda (although, realistically, that was never going to happen) or sailed the Greek Islands on a super-yacht. And, my poor mum. It was bad enough she had to bury one child. No one ever expects that, yet here we were, ten years later, almost to the day, and she was about to do the same with her second.

And, my dad. My poor dad. I knew he'd bury himself in lawsuits and Ziggy's dodgy legal dealings, but deep down, I knew this would break him.

That made me sad.

I thought of Drew, too.

And Miss Miranda.

I thought of everything that made life worth living; salted caramel ice cream, weekend Netflix binges, thunderstorms, playing backgammon with my mum, wrapping Christmas presents and watching Carols in the Domain, kitten purrs, singing to your favorite song, the smell of the ocean, first kisses.

I was going to miss all that—hard.

But the inky darkness was right there, beckoning, calling my name, inviting me into its velvety embrace.

"What have you done, Sonny? What have you done?" Vincent's voice echoed through the hall, which had fallen eerily silent. It was like there'd been a collective *shoosh*, so everyone could savor the final moments of my short, but somehow significant existence. Significant to them, at least.

"What you didn't have the strength to do yourself," Sonny said with an edge of disgust in his voice. I realized then, there was a lot about him I didn't know. I didn't know his shoe size or how he took his tea. I didn't know his favorite song, and I certainly didn't know he was capable of killing me.

I guess it didn't matter anymore. I'd never find out if he preferred *Friends* or *Seinfeld*. Or if he listened to true crime podcasts at bedtime, like me.

Shame, really, because I was beginning to think we could have had something.

"Clarissa." Azrael's voice was gentle and melodic. "It's time."

"I know," I said. "I'm just not ready."

"You are. You've always been ready."

"I haven't done everything I wanted to do yet," I whispered. "I haven't even gotten that unicorn tattoo I always wanted."

"That tattoo was always a crappy idea," Azrael said. "You've lived a good life. That's all that matters." He stroked my hair. "You deserve to be in a better place."

"Will I see you there? Where I'm going, I mean?"

Azrael shook his head. "No. Our journey ends when you arrive in the after world," he said.

"Oh." That made my heart ache, and not because of the silver dagger. Azrael was my friend—my best friend. I was going to miss him. "Will you look after Miss Miranda for me? Make sure she's okay?"

"She hates my guts," he said, smiling through watery eyes.

"No, she doesn't. She just doesn't...doesn't...know... you...yet."

A shadow fell over us and I looked up to see Sonny staring down at me. It was like looking into a stranger's eyes. Cold, emotionless. After a moment, Sonny turned his back on me, and stalked out of the great hall.

Boy, did I sure know how to pick 'em. At that moment, Robbie the klepto I dated for nine months didn't seem so bad, and he's the one who'd stolen my Beamer.

Azrael rocked my body back and forth, sobbing ever so quietly, as I slipped into the darkness and the comfort of death's warm embrace.

I thought of my parents.

And I thought of Poppy.

And Miss Miranda, and that really good cheese I'd eaten in Auckland; the Drunken Nanny Black Tie Petite—it won the Puhoi Valley Cheese Champion of Champions Cheese Award. So good.

And then I thought of nothing at all.

TO BE CONTINUED...

If you enjoyed Cross My Werewolf Heart *and would like to read the second instalment in the trilogy, flip to the next page to read the blurb for* Cross My Werewolf Heart: Hope Not to Die. *All three books are out now, so you can head to your favorite retailer to keep reading.*

Cross My Werewolf Heart Hope Not to Die...Again

"For some reason, I thought heaven would look more, I don't know, heavenly."
—Clarissa Hunt, Cross My Werewolf Heart: Hope Not to Die...Again.

•

I was wrong. It could get worse. It could get a whole lot worse... And it did.

Not only has Alpha Werewolf, Silvio De Benedetto disappeared, but now I'm facing the prospect of my first full moon with a werewolf heart.

Would I transform into a snarling, drooling monster and tear up the town—literally? Or would I discover an exciting new paranormal ability to go along with the half dozen or so I'd already developed?

Things get more complicated when I steal my best friend's car following a minor (read: major) personal crisis, and get kidnapped by a coven of disgusting vampires, hell-bent in claiming the hefty blood bounty on my head.

How? How do I keep getting into these ridiculously dangerous situations, when all I want to do is go back to my nice, normal life?

What did I ever do?

Something tells me, though, finally getting to the bottom of the whole saga, and discovering what a werewolf heart truly means for my future, the nice, normal life I long to return to is nothing more than a distant memory.

•

Cross My Werewolf Heart: Hope Not to Die...Again is the thrilling conclusion to the fast-paced, raucously funny and wildly unpredictable Cross My Werewolf Heart trilogy, set in the fantastical world of #fangsfurandfreaks

But don't expect full closure at the end of this book. Nah-uh! There are still plenty of questions surrounding the origin of Clarissa's werewolf heart, and the role it plays in her past, present, and future.

So, keep an eye out for the next exciting instalment in the Werewolf Heart paranormal adventure series, Break My Werewolf Heart, hitting bookshelves and online stores Halloween 2024!

ABOUT THE AUTHOR

Esther Del Zuanne is a mentor and communications specialist who love, love, loves to write lively, paranormal romantic comedies. Her heroines are bold and brash with boundless energy and tonnes of pizazz - and a dash of sass thrown in for good measure. Her heroes are daring, brave, super-sexy and oh, so, cheeky... Impossible to resist and easy to love.

Esther's debut *Cross My Werewolf Heart* trilogy, is the first in her **#fangsfurandfreaks** series, based on the misadventures of Clarissa Hunt and the mysterious Patrons of Order - keepers of the thin veneer that separates humanity from the seething supernatural world on its doorstep.

When she's not writing about things that go bump and growl in the night, Esther spends her time going to rock concerts, cruising **realestate.com** for beach-front properties she'll never afford, and watching her favourite horror movies over and over and over again.

She's been married to the Rock God since 1996 and lives in Melbourne, Australia, with two fur babies, waaaaay too many cushions (or so she's been told) and an embarrassing collection of Buffy the Vampire Slayer memorabilia.

Esther also loves hearing from readers and other writers. You can find all her contact details, social media links and sign up for her newsletter, by visiting **estherdelzuanne.com**